THE AMENDMENT

AN ARRANGEMENT NOVEL

KIERSTEN MODGLIN

KIERSTEN
MODGLIN

Cover Design by Kiersten Modglin
Copy Editing by Three Owls Editing
Proofreading by My Brother's Editor
Formatting by Kiersten Modglin
Copyright © 2021 by Kiersten Modglin
All rights reserved.

First Print and Electronic Edition: 2022
kierstenmodglinauthor.com

This one's for all the fans who trusted me to tell the last crazy story...and then begged for another.

AUTHOR'S NOTE

Dear Reader,

Thank you for picking up this book! THE AMEND-MENT is the completely twisted sequel to my domestic thriller, THE ARRANGEMENT. In order to fully understand the events in this book, it's important that you start at the beginning. If you haven't had a chance to read THE ARRANGEMENT, start there: http://mybook.to/arrangement, then come back here for the rest of the dark and scandalous story.

Thanks so much for your support. I hope you love every thrilling moment!

XO,

Kiersten

CHAPTER ONE

AINSLEY

My husband was a monster.

It was something I'd come to accept over the years.

It could also be argued, I supposed, that I was equally monstrous. Some of the things I've done to keep our family together were questionable, morally gray, I would say. But it was all a matter of opinion.

What mattered was that it worked.

I fixed us.

At least, I would.

We were a work in progress. Aren't we all?

I glanced over to the passenger seat where Peter sat, fidgeting with the collar of his shirt.

I swatted his hand. "Leave it alone."

His brow rose just a hair, but he didn't bother arguing. Lately, he didn't argue with anything I said. He'd become my lapdog, dutifully doing whatever I needed or whatever I said.

I thought it was what I wanted.

A quiet coexistence.

But, truth be told, I missed the spark I used to see in his eyes. I missed who we used to be… Before.

Before our world changed.

Before he found out I knew his secrets.

My latest mission was to bring that version of my husband back.

Whatever it took.

"Are you sure about this?" he asked, twisting his wedding band around his finger.

"Of course I am. Why?" I pulled the car into the paved parking lot of our new therapist's office.

He shook his head, staring at the glass door with her name on it.

Joanna St. James, LMFT

"I'm just not sure we're *marriage counseling* people. She's going to see right through us."

I shut the car off, resting my hands in my lap. "Don't be ridiculous. What exactly are *marriage counseling* people, Peter?"

He practically flinched as I said his name, though I'd thought I was speaking gently. "Just forget it. Let's go in."

I reached for his hand as he started to open the door, and he stopped, glancing over at me. "I want to do this because I want to fix us. You know that. I want to rebuild our trust."

His stony expression softened. "I want that, too. You know I do. It's just…" He sighed, looking back at the office door through the windshield. "I don't know what

2

we'll even talk about. Our problems aren't exactly normal."

He winced as he said it, and I let his words wash over me. We sat in silence for a moment, and when he finally looked up at me, a laugh slipped through my lips.

Then more laughter.

Soon, he'd joined me. I felt the stress leaving my shoulders as we laughed together at the ridiculousness of our situation and the truth of his words.

"That just might be the understatement of the century," I said, when I'd finally caught my breath. He was smiling at me, and I slid my hand down his arm and into his palm, squeezing it gently. "Look, I know this will be… complicated. But we'll handle it. We always do." He still didn't look convinced. Didn't want to admit to his issues and how they were affecting us. "We'll just talk to her. It's only one hour. If things go wrong, we won't go back. We'll have our answer. But we have to do this, Peter. We have to. Otherwise, we're just giving up and hoping for the best."

He sighed again, though less begrudgingly. "Okay, let's get this over with."

Though I didn't appreciate the attitude, I released his hand and stepped from the car. We walked together in silence toward the door, and he held it open for me to pass through.

The lobby was small and quaint, a neutral palette of cream and gray. The woman behind a small, natural wooden desk in the corner was talking into a headset. She smiled at us, holding a finger up briefly.

"Okay, I'll let her know. I've got you down for the

fourth." She paused. "Mhm. You bet." Another pause as I felt Peter's fingers lace through mine. I smoothed down a piece of my hair out of nervous habit. "Okay. Buh-bye." She looked up at us. "I'm sorry about that. How can I help you?"

"We've got a one o'clock with Joanna," I told her.

She typed something into the desktop in front of her, nodding. "You're the Greens?"

I smiled at the familiar fake name. "Yes."

"Okay, I've got you checked in. She should be right out." The woman stood, gesturing toward a matching set of gray sofas behind us. "Feel free to have a seat while you wait. Can I get you anything? Water? Coffee? Soda?"

"No, thank you," I said.

At the same time, Peter said, "Coffee would be fine."

"Of course. Be right back." She nodded, disappearing around the corner. Moments later, she returned with a paper cup. "It's hot. I just made a fresh pot. I left room in case you'd like to add cream or sugar." She pointed to a small table on the far side of the room that had powdered creamer, various packs of sweetener, and black stirrers just as the door to our left opened.

"Okay, guys, I'll see you next week. You have your homework." I turned my head to look at the voice, spying two men exiting the office.

I recognized Joanna from her pictures. She was a bit older than us, maybe early fifties, with stark black hair and thick-framed glasses. She was beautiful—even more so than I'd imagined from her pictures—and she moved with an easy elegance that felt out of place in the small office.

As she waved goodbye to the couple, I noted one's puffy, red eyes and the other's grim expression. I tried to picture Peter and me leaving the same way in exactly an hour—it seemed ridiculous.

Once the door had shut behind them, she turned her attention to us and we stood. "Are you Pete and Annie?"

"Yes," Peter confirmed, glancing at me, though I kept my attention trained on her.

"I'm Joanna. It's nice to meet you both. Come on in." She pushed the door behind her back a bit and allowed us into her office. Once we were inside, she shut it again, closing us into a cocoon of silence.

The walls of the large room were painted a warm cream color, with paintings of plants here and there. In the center of the space were two gray sofas that matched the ones in the lobby, sitting directly across from each other, and an off-white chair at one end, creating a sort of U shape.

The entire far wall was lined with windows, giving a clear view into a courtyard filled with a meticulously kept garden. Farther back, I could see the mostly empty parking lot and our car waiting for us.

We stopped awkwardly just before the sofas, and she moved around us, smiling as she gestured for us to take a seat. Once we had, she sat down in the chair, folding one leg over the other and leaning backward.

"So..." Her smile was warm but cautious. I watched her gaze trailing over us, attempting to read us, trying to gain perspective and insights from the way my shoulders tensed or how Peter gripped his knees.

I knew what she was doing—could see straight through it. But she'd never get the truth about us.

She'd get what we gave her and nothing else.

"Would you like to tell me what brought you here today?"

Peter glanced at me cautiously, and I scooted forward just a hair. He needed me to speak for us, so I would. "Well, we've been having some problems in our marriage. We tried counseling before, but it didn't seem to work."

"How long were you in counseling previously?"

"Six months?" I asked, though I knew that was it exactly. Six months for me, at least. Peter had shown up to less than half the sessions before I'd given up and canceled any future ones.

"I see." She spoke slowly. "Well, it's normal for couples to try out different therapists and therapy methods before they find the one that's right for them." She clasped her hands together in front of her. "I'm really glad you're here." Then her eyes fell to Peter.

"Pete, why do *you* think you're here?"

He readjusted in his seat, shifting the coffee cup from one hand to the other, obviously uncomfortable with being put on the spot. I willed him to pull it together, keeping a smile plastered on my face. "Um, well, we've been married for nearly twenty years, our kids are growing up, and we're…" He looked at me.

"Pete," Joanna said, somewhat sternly, pulling his attention back to her. I liked her. "Tell me. Tell me what *you* think. You don't have to get Annie's opinion on that."

Or…maybe I didn't like her so much. Something about

the way she said my name told me she'd already pegged me as controlling. Manipulative, maybe.

If she only knew...

There was only one true bad guy in this room.

"We're growing apart, I guess. It's been hard. Like she said, we've tried counseling and date nights and..." He was going to slip up, but he caught himself. "Well, I guess one of the biggest issues is that I've become somewhat addicted to fencing. And Annie wants me to stop."

Fencing.

The word we'd come up with to discuss Peter's discretions in our session. If she was surprised, she hid it well. "*Fencing?* Interesting. Tell me more about that, Annie."

She tossed the figurative ball back to my court, and I smiled. "Well, for one, it's not entirely about the fencing." I nodded in his direction slowly. "It's more how obsessed Pete has become with it. He lies to me about where he is and what he's doing, which certainly puts a strain on our trust—"

She held up a hand, cutting me off. "We're talking about fencing, as in the sport—swords and metal mesh masks, right?" Her hand was held in front of her face.

"Yes, that's right. Pete did it a bit in college, but then gave it up when we'd gotten married. But lately, he's gone back to it."

"I see... And Pete, why do you feel the need to lie about it?"

I couldn't hide my smile as I looked his way, watching him physically squirm. He crossed one leg over the other, then uncrossed it, switching legs just to avoid eye contact. "I guess I'm embarrassed by it."

"Why should you be?" she coaxed.

"Well, for one thing, growing up, I was always made to feel like I needed to be doing something *manly*, you know? And fencing makes me feel...good. But I know it's not really something most people approve of."

"By that, you mean Annie doesn't approve?"

He nodded, and she looked at me again. "Annie, what is it about Peter's fencing that you don't approve of? Is it just the lying and sneaking around?"

"I'll be honest and say I had a really hard time with the fencing in the beginning. I just didn't understand it. It...it scared me a little. But then, I mean, really, the lying has become the biggest issue, yes. I'm trying to be understanding about the rest. I don't like secrets. I want to know what my husband is up to, and I don't understand why he has to lie to me," I said firmly.

"I see." She was still for a moment, staring at us with intense concentration. "Have you tried to explain to Pete what it is about the sport that bothers you? Have you had a bad experience with it personally? What do you think it is about fencing that caused you to have such a reaction to it in the beginning?"

I pressed my lips together, trying to work out my answer in my head before I gave it. "The violence of it. The anger involved... He didn't tell me it was something he was interested in, either, not when we met, or even after we'd been married. I didn't know until I caught him one night when he'd said he was working late."

"So, Pete, you felt the need to hide something you were passionate about even before Annie told you she disapproved. Why do you think that is?"

"I know my wife. I knew she wouldn't approve," he said simply.

I could already feel her judgment of me, but she didn't look my way. Not yet. She was too busy feeling sorry for my husband.

He was good at that.

No one had ever seen him for what he was until it was smacking them in the face, myself included.

"Have there been other things she hasn't approved of?"

"No, I—"

She cut me off, holding a finger up. "Annie, let's let Pete talk and then you'll get a turn to respond." Leaning forward in her chair slightly, as if he were a shy child she was having to coax out of hiding, she went on. "Pete?"

I held my breath, waiting for him to respond. When he finally did, I released a quiet sigh of relief.

"No, um, Ains—Annie is great. It's me. The problem is, and always has been, me."

She nodded, as if she had us all figured out. "Okay, I'd like to dig into why you feel that way. These things are very rarely one sided. But, before we do that, I'd like to hear from you, Annie. How do you feel when you hear Pete speak that way? Do you agree with him? Or do you think you both share the blame?"

I knew what she wanted me to say, but that wasn't the truth. I wasn't at fault or to blame. This was all Peter. Everything that had gone wrong in our lives could be traced back to Peter.

"Obviously, we're both to blame, but this all started when he began sneaking around."

9

"Do you have any idea why he might've felt the need to sneak around?"

"No," I said firmly. "I honestly don't. I've been here for him—"

"Talk to him," she said, gesturing toward my husband. "Tell him what you're telling me. *I've been there for you—*"

I turned toward him, feeling as if I were putting on a performance. "I've been there for you through everything. And yet, you still act like I'm the enemy."

"How does that make you feel, Annie?" she asked from her side of the room.

"Alone," I said, surprising myself with a completely honest answer. "Helpless. Like you don't trust me."

Peter's eyes were zeroed in on mine, glassy and serious. "I do trust you—"

"Pete, how does that make you feel? To hear how your actions are affecting Annie?"

"Shitty," he said. "Guilty." Then, his eyes widened only slightly, as if he'd realized something. "Alone."

From across the room, Joanna sat back in her chair with a weighty breath. "And there, you see, you're both working from a similar place. The fear of being alone is driving you to do things that's only pushing your partner away. Instead of working together, you're trying to protect yourselves and each other, to the detriment of your marriage."

Our trance seemed to break, both of us blinking and turning to meet her eyes. "Do you think you can help us?" Peter asked anxiously, then gave a dry laugh. "I mean, are we a lost cause?"

"I can only help you as much as you want to be helped.

But, if you're willing to put in the work, to be completely honest with me, and with each other, I think there's no limit to what we can do in this room. It all depends on you."

I felt a smile growing on my lips as Peter's hand slipped into mine.

"We'll do whatever it takes," I vowed, my heart thudding in my chest.

She smiled back at us, believing our every word.

Thirty minutes later, we made our way back to the car and slid in without a word. Peter held a paper with our *homework*—tell our partner how their actions make us feel at least once a day and tell our partner something we appreciate about them once a day—on it.

I glanced over at him, watching his expression grow dark.

Haunted.

Excited.

"So," he said, obviously fighting against the joy he felt, "are we going to kill her?"

CHAPTER TWO

PETER

TWO MONTHS EARLIER

I stared at my wife across the kitchen table, the note I'd found in my bag lying between us.

It felt right somehow, that this was where it would end for us. Since this was where it had all begun just months before. When we'd agreed to the arrangement.

When I had no idea what I was agreeing to.

"How long have you known?" I asked, running a hand through my hair. I needed to do damage control, but I had no idea how to. How much did she know? Was there any use trying to lie or cover it up?

"How long has it been going on?" she retorted.

"Ainsley, this isn't some game. What you've done—"

Her jaw dropped open. "What *I've* done? Oh, that's rich coming from you. All I've done is clean up your mess again and again." She pounded her fist on the table. "And, frankly, I'm tired of it."

"So, what are you saying? Are you going to turn me

in?" My blood ran cold at the thought. She was manipulative, but she wasn't evil…was she? I couldn't believe she'd actually go to the police.

She scoffed. "And let our children find out what you've done? Our community?" I watched as her hands folded in front of her carefully, her long, thin fingers gracefully intertwined. "No, I won't be doing that. Besides, from here on out, there will be nothing to tell me that I won't already know."

"Meaning what?"

"Why were you going into the bag, Peter? What did you do now?"

My stomach clenched. "I—*nothing.*"

"You only go into that room, into that bag, when you've hurt someone new. So, who was she? How far did you go?"

She was asking me about the darkest moments of my life so blatantly. It was painful and surreal, knowing the thing I'd tried to keep hidden for so long—the thing I'd thought I *had* kept hidden—wasn't hidden at all. But rather, she'd known all along.

I should've known. Ainsley was always one step ahead of me.

She always knew.

Always.

"Ainsley, please, I didn't… I didn't do anything. I won't. I don't know what you think you—" I was breathless, unable to meet her eye. Illiana's pearl bracelet still rested in my pocket.

"I can find out, you know. But it's better if you tell me."

I wanted to ask how she could find out, but in truth, it

didn't matter. She wasn't bluffing, and we both knew it. "I'm not the same man I was."

"You're a killer, Peter." She spat it out, finally laying the truth on the table. "A rapist. A liar. *A monster.* You hurt people. You've hurt me."

I rested my face in my palms, tears stinging my eyes. "I don't mean to do it."

"Which part?"

"Any of it!"

She shoved back from the table, stalking across the room toward the pitcher of lemonade she'd made just hours before. She pulled a bottle of vodka from the shelf above the refrigerator and added it to her drink. "It's not like you tripped and fell into it. Like they had a job fair and you didn't know what you were signing up for. You can never take responsibility for anything, can you?"

"You don't understand—"

"No, here's what I understand: you meant to do it. You always mean to do it. The first time I caught you was when Maisy was a baby."

"What?" It wasn't possible. How could she have looked me in the eyes all this time, knowing what she knew?

"You were supposed to be going out with Seth for the night, but when I called over to see if Glennon wanted to visit, she said she was watching some new documentary *with Seth*. I knew you'd lied. So, the next time you said you were going out, I followed you." She made her way back to the table and took a seat, and I wondered if my face looked as pale as it felt. I was sure I was going to pass out.

"I thought you were having an affair. I watched you hitting on a woman in a bar. Here I was, still recovering from childbirth, and you were out on a date. But, just before I started to confront you, I watched you slip something in her drink." She sprinkled her fingers over her own drink, acting out my motions.

Maybe I wouldn't pass out, but I was certain I was going to be sick.

"Ainsley, I—" She waited, staring at me suspiciously, but we both knew there was nothing I could say that would make this better. "I'm sorry. I'm so sorry."

"I felt you pulling away from me back then. I knew something wasn't right. But I never thought... I never dreamed you could be..." She couldn't bring herself to say it again. Lifting the glass to her lips, she took another sip. "By the time I saw you for who you were, it was too late. I had three babies with you. We had a life. A home. Friends. I couldn't just throw that all away. I thought if I did more, if I tried harder, that you would realize what you had. But you never did. Sometimes we'd go months, years even, when things felt okay. But then, you'd start sneaking around again, start spacing out, lying. No matter what I did, it was never enough to bring you back to me."

"This has nothing to do with you. Do you hear me? It's not you. It's me." I smacked a fist into my chest. "I'm broken, Ainsley. I can't explain it. I can't... It doesn't make sense. Not even to me. I love you. I love our kids. I don't want to be this person." I reached across the table, touching her hand gently, but she pulled it back.

"But you *are* this person, Peter. At least, half of you is. And, try as I might, I can't figure out how to hang on to just the half of you that doesn't hurt people—myself included."

My mouth was too dry. I licked my lips, trying to think. Trying to come up with something—anything—to say to make this better. "Look, I can't take back what I've done, but I can stop. I promise you I can. I haven't hurt anyone in more than a year."

"You're still lying to me," she said pointedly.

"What are you talking about? I'm not!"

"Then why were you in the room?"

"I..." I could try to lie, I knew. But what if she found out? Now was my chance to come clean about it all. To lay myself bare and let her decide if she could handle the real me.

A fleeting thought crossed my mind: what if she couldn't?

What if she couldn't handle who I was?

Would I have to...

No, the thought was impossible. I'd sooner turn myself in than ever harm Ainsley. I loved her too much.

"I can just go in there and look, you know. You thought you were so clever having that room built, didn't you? Did you really think I wouldn't find out why you were spending so much time in the garage? You're not exactly a handyman, Peter. Eventually, you had to know I'd wonder why you were sneaking out in the middle of the night. And the code, the pattern for the kids' birthdays, was easy enough to guess." She tutted. "You're predictable, Peter, even when you shock me."

She'd find nothing if she went and looked, so I was tempted to invite her to do so. The bracelet remained safely with me, and there was nothing else to clue her in

16

about Illiana, but part of me wanted to admit the truth. She knew just about everything, yet she was still here.

"Are you planning to leave me?" I asked, swiping my sweaty palms across my pants. I wasn't sure I'd be able to hear her answer over the sound of my racing heart. I wasn't sure I wanted to.

"You should know by now that's not an option," she replied. "We're in this together. You and me. But you promised no more secrets, and you broke that promise. So—" She looked away, shaking her head. "I'm not sure what to do with you."

"I want to be honest with you, Ainsley, I do. I just hate myself. I don't know how you can look at me, knowing what I've done. What I've—"

She slammed her palm down on the table, startling me. "The pity party is officially over. I saved you, Peter. I sent the cops on Stefan's trail. I gave them all the evidence they'd need to fill in the blanks for him being the serial killer. *I saved you.* I own you. But you *will not* lie to me. Whatever you've got going on—however dark—as long as you're honest with me, I promise you we can get through it. But you have to tell me the truth. About everything. The kids are gone for the night; this is our chance to lay it all out once and for all."

"What do you want to know?"

"Everything. How it started. Why you went into that room tonight. Who else knows about this."

I nodded, my hands trembling. "Okay, fine."

"Start talking."

"I, um…" I ran a hand through my hair, trying to think. "Well, it started in college. When my parents got divorced.

It's not an excuse, but...I was in a dark place. There was this guy—my roommate. It was just something he did. It wasn't... I mean, I never started out planning to hurt anyone, you know? I needed to let off steam, and it just happened." Her face was still and solemn as she waited for me to continue. "I needed to feel in control of something. And, I did. I didn't...it was never about the women. It was always about me. And then...then I met you."

Her head tilted to the side as if something had just occurred to her. "Wait, was I supposed to be one of your victims?"

A lump formed in my throat as I recalled the night I met her. The drugs in my pocket, just waiting to be used. But something about her had stopped me. She was bossy, hard to please. She didn't laugh at all my jokes like the others had, didn't hang all over me as we danced. In fact, she'd ignored me most of the night, if memory served. I liked that. Craved it. In some sick way, I wanted someone who'd make me work to please them. Someone who could point me in a direction—any direction—when I felt so utterly lost and alone.

"Peter," she snapped, still waiting for an answer.

"Sorry. You were...yes." Honesty was harder than I'd expected. If this was a surprise, she didn't react. "But I couldn't go through with it. I fell for you so fast, Ains. I loved you that night, I've told you that. And I stopped. From the moment we met, I never hurt anyone else. You were all I needed."

She pursed her lips. "Until I stopped being enough."

"I've told you, it had nothing to do with you." She looked unconvinced, so I went on. "It was me. This brokenness inside me. I'd kept it at bay for so long, but I couldn't do it any longer. The first time was this one night...after one of our biggest fights." I tried to bring back the memory I'd spent so long trying to repress. "It was when Lae Haer was struggling financially. Before we brought Beckman in, before his investment. We'd been fighting and drinking, and I felt like everything was all my fault. Like I couldn't do anything right. I couldn't provide for you. I couldn't take care of you and the kids."

"I remember that fight," she said softly, staring off into space. "You were gone for the night. You said you'd slept at the office."

One of my many lies.

"Yeah. I just couldn't believe I'd let myself slip. Of all the things I'd done, I'd never cheated on you before. You'd kept me sober. Because this is an addiction, Ainsley. It's the only way I know how to describe it. The pull...the need to do it, it's unlike anything I could try to explain. I'd been clean for all those years, but I slipped. I was like an addict, going back to the thing that always managed to make me feel...good, numb, I don't know. It made me feel something when nothing else would. And then I found myself slipping more and more. No matter how hard I tried to stop, no matter how badly I wanted to tell you the truth, I couldn't. I couldn't be honest, because I thought I'd lose you. I deserve to lose you." My voice cracked as I said it, but it was the truth. What I couldn't understand was why she was still there in the first place.

"But if you weren't killing people when we got married and built the house, why did you have the room

19

built in the first place?" she asked, her eyes inquisitive rather than judging.

Why was she so perfect?

"I don't know." I looked away, toward the dark window. If someone were to look in at us, we'd look like an average couple having a boring conversation over a mostly empty dinner table. It amazed me the secrets you could hide by appearing average. "I guess it was just sort of a backup plan. Just in case." I wasn't sure if she believed me, despite it being the truth, so I added, "Look, I'm very clear about who I am. No matter how badly I want to be better for you. I've always known deep down that I'm not a good guy. I knew if I ever relapsed, I'd need a place to hide the bodies. I hoped I'd never have to use it, but I needed somewhere to go, just in case."

"Creating a plan B was your problem, Peter. Somehow, creating a plan B always makes certain that we'll need to use it."

"I realize that now."

"So why did you go in the room tonight? I'm giving you one chance to tell me the truth." As if to prove her point, she took another sip of her drink and placed her hand on the edge of the table, ready to stand.

"Illiana," I blurted out. Shoving my hand in my pocket, I produced her bracelet. "I took care of her."

She stared at the bracelet with an expression I couldn't read. Was it horror or pride? "You..."

"I didn't rape her." I scowled. "I killed her. I didn't have a choice. She put us all in danger. She had to go."

Slowly, her eyes lifted to meet mine. "What did you do with her body?"

"She's with him," I said simply. "It's all taken care of."

I saw a flicker of something in her expression. Something warm. Appreciative. I'd done the right thing, even if it was awful. "And that's hers?"

"I was going to put it in the bag."

"Why the souvenirs?" she asked.

"I don't know." My shoulders dropped. "I wish I did. It's like...sometimes, after it happens, I can't remember if it was real or if it was all a dream. Collecting something from them...it keeps me planted in reality. It reminds me they were real."

She looked away, and I wondered if I'd crossed a line. Any semblance of warmth that had been present moments ago was now gone.

"I'm done with all of that, though. I promise you I am. Now that you know, now that I can talk to you, you can help me."

"But will I ever be enough for you, Peter? Even when you weren't killing... What about Seth? How many others have there been that were just affairs? In some sick way, I can almost look past the murders. But the affairs are different. They're personal."

Seth.

I grimaced, looking down. "It's not like that."

"You said it was different with him. Was he the only one?"

"Yes," I blurted out. "Look, Seth never knew the extent of what I've done. He... He caught me out with a woman. *Once.* I was terrified he was going to tell Glennon. And I knew then it would only be a matter of time before it got back to you. So, I tried to buy myself time by telling him

21

that we'd had a rocky few months. That's when he told me the truth about his marriage to Glennon. I knew the only way to keep him quiet, to be sure that he wouldn't tell Glennon, or you, was to start seeing him. To convince him that I was falling for him."

"So it was all a lie? You didn't have feelings for him?"

"Never more than just as a friend. I thought I was doing what I needed to in order to keep you safe and happy. I convinced him I was confused... He was trying to help me figure out my sexuality. With his shitbag parents, he understood that more than most. Eventually, I was going to tell him that I wanted to stay with you. But Glennon caught us together before I had the chance. She was supposed to be gone for a weekend, but she came home early. That's when she gave me the ultimatum to tell you, or she would. And...well, you know the rest."

She nodded, but she still wasn't looking at me. "You really hurt Seth. And me. And Glennon."

"I know that," I admitted, reaching for her hand again. To my surprise, she didn't pull it away. "But it was all to save our marriage. You may not see it that way, but it was always to protect you from who I was. Because despite everything, I'm crazy about you, Ainsley. I want to be with you. I want to be everything you deserve. Maybe I went about it the wrong way, but it's always been with earnest intentions."

Her gaze flicked to me finally, and I saw a hint of tears in her eyes.

"Please don't cry..."

She dusted her cheeks quickly, drawing her lips inward with a sniff. "I'm just processing."

"None of this is your fault—"

"I know that," she cut me off.

"And I want to get better—"

"You will." She was certain, and for that, I was grateful. "I'm going to help you, Peter. I thought I was helping you with the arrangement. I thought it would give you the freedom you needed, while also giving you a chance to come clean about everything. But it didn't work. Not completely. In the end, after every chance I gave you, I still had to tell you I knew the truth. But now, now that it's all out there, we can move forward. I can fix this. Us."

As much as I wanted her to fix it, I couldn't help thinking about the last time she'd had to fix something for me.

That particular fix was still decaying under the freshly poured patio.

"I'll do anything you want," I heard myself saying. "I just don't want to lose you."

"You won't." She slid her hand away from mine. "It's all going to be okay."

The woman I knew was back. The one I'd fallen in love with. The nonsense and pain had fallen away, and the cool, collected version of her had returned. I had no doubt that if anyone could fix me, it was Ainsley.

"We just need to change up the rules a bit," she said, a small smile on her lips.

"What do you mean?"

"Give me a bit to think on it." She pushed away from the table. "I'm going to take a shower. Take care of the bracelet while I'm gone."

I stared at the bracelet—lying there, taunting me—and

swallowed. Before she'd departed the room, she turned to face me one last time.

"Oh, and Peter?"

"Yeah?"

"Are there any other secrets you need to tell me? Anything I should know?"

My response was instant. A vow. A lie. "No. You know everything."

Her lips upturned into what should've been a smile, but looked cruel instead. "Good," she purred. "Because if you ever lie to me again, the next body in our freezer will be yours."

CHAPTER THREE

AINSLEY

I wasn't sure how I was going to handle the revelation about Peter. I'd known enough before, but now that I knew everything, it was as if I'd learned it all again. The pain was fresh, the shock very real.

I told myself I could forgive him for anything, but now, I just didn't know if that was true. I wanted to save him. To protect him from himself, but was that possible?

I'd failed before.

Not just with Peter. There had been others.

One other, specifically.

But that was the past. Peter wasn't Ryan. This was different. *We* were different. I loved him more than I could say, and he loved me back. I wouldn't fail to save him.

I couldn't.

I wasn't sure I'd survive it—

A knock at the door caused me to jolt.

"What?" I shouted over the sound of the water.

"It's Maisy," Peter said, his voice wary. The anger dissipated instantly, and I shut the water off, reaching for a towel and scrambling out of the shower.

"What is it? Is she okay?"

He jiggled the door handle. "She's sick. Bailey's mom just called. Do you want me to go get her?"

"No," I said, too quickly. "No. I'm coming with you." I dried my body quickly before opening the bathroom door and darting down the hall toward our room. Peter gave my body an appreciative glance, but I pretended not to notice. I couldn't think of him in that way. Not now. We needed to get to our little girl.

She needed us.

In the bedroom, I dropped the towel, turning away from him as I pulled on my clothes and tied my hair back out of my face. Once I was dressed, I looked at him.

"Did you get rid of it?"

"It's gone." He patted his pocket, as if to prove a point.

"Good. We should stop by the pharmacy and pick her up some medicine. Did Amber say what was wrong with her?"

"Sounds like a stomach bug. Maisy mentioned there's been one going around."

"We'll need crackers and broth, then. And ginger ale." I rattled off the list, counting them off on my fingers. I might as well have kept them in my head; it wasn't as if I could count on Peter to remember what I was saying.

I tugged on my shoes and headed for the door. "Let's go."

He was behind me as we made our way toward the garage. I checked to be sure he'd moved the shelf back to cover the secret room—not that he had ever forgotten that—and climbed into the driver's seat.

"I'm texting her to let her know we're leaving now," he said.

I didn't ask if he meant Amber or Maisy. I didn't ask anything. My mind was focused on the to-do list forming in my head.

There was so much I still needed to say to my husband, but none of it mattered. I needed to get to my child.

Like so much else in my life, in our marriage, everything else could wait.

It's what a good mother would do.

CHAPTER FOUR

PETER

We pulled into the garage an hour and a half later with Maisy curled in the back seat, her legs tucked up in front of her. She'd been whimpering most of the way, clutching for dear life to the spare pitcher Amber had given her.

We weren't sure if it was a stomach bug or something she'd eaten, but whatever it was had her vomiting every hour or so. Every window in the car was rolled down in an attempt to alleviate the putrid smell.

When Ainsley parked the car, I slid out of my side door, hurrying to scoop Maisy up and carry her inside. Ainsley was just behind me, carrying the bag from the grocery store we'd stopped at to stock up on whatever our daughter might need.

This was when we were at our best—Ains and I. When we had to work together as a team, no matter the reason, we fired on all cylinders. It was why we were so good. So much of our life had been bouncing from one situation to the next. One problem after the other: sick kids, work emergencies, her parents' divorce, Glennon getting cancer, her grandfather's dementia. We'd been in crisis mode for so long, sometimes I wondered if we even remembered how to be normal.

Then again, what was normal anyway?

Actually, now that I thought about it, the most *normal* time in our marriage had also been the most drab. Perhaps the most problematic.

It was that period of time that led us to try the arrangement in the first place.

At least, that was what Ainsley had let me believe in the beginning.

I placed Maisy in her bed, tugging her shoes off her feet and pulling the comforter around her shoulders. Ainsley was just behind me, pouring her a glass of ginger ale and placing a plate of crackers next to it.

"Get a washcloth," she instructed, lowering herself next to Maisy as she rubbed her cheeks carefully.

I did as I was told, returning moments later and handing it over. Ainsley was helping her out of her clothes as Maisy whined.

"Come on now, sweetheart, you'll feel better once you've changed." She tossed the clothes next to her on the floor and held out a hand for the washcloth. When I handed it to her, I knew I'd done something wrong. Her face contorted, eyes rolling. "Peter, did you wet this?"

"You didn't say..."

She shoved it back toward me. "Warm water. For her head." I turned away from her, cloth in hand, and retreated toward the bathroom again. When I came back, Ainsley had Maisy dressed in her pajamas. She took the washcloth from me and used it to stroke Maisy's fore-head. "Is there anything else we can get you, baby?" she cooed. I couldn't remember the last time she'd talked to me that way.

Maisy shook her head. "Thanks, Momma."

"I'll just be down the hall," she said.

"Try to get some rest," I chimed in.

With that, we backed out of the room, watching as Maisy pulled the comforter up around her chin. Once we were safely in the hall, Ainsley nodded at me.

A confirmation that it was all going to be okay.

"I need a drink," she said simply, turning to walk toward the kitchen. As she did, I reached into my pocket and checked my phone. It had gone off on the drive home, but I'd been too preoccupied to check it at the time.

When I spied the name on my screen, my stomach tightened instinctively.

It had been years since he'd called me on my personal phone, even longer since I'd answered. What could he possibly want now?

We'd long since severed ties personally, choosing only to continue our semblance of a relationship professionally.

Even that was a stretch.

I shoved the phone back into my pocket, trying to tamp down the curiosity as I made my way into the kitchen.

I had enough on my plate. Whatever he wanted, it would have to wait.

Always one crisis to the next.

CHAPTER FIVE

AINSLEY

I stayed home with Maisy the next day, periodically refilling her soup and drink. While she was sleeping, I scrubbed and sanitized every inch of our house, washing all the bedding and shampooing all the carpets.

If I didn't get ahead of it, the sickness would wash through our house like the plague, taking each of us out for a few days. If I managed to catch it, the family would fall apart. Without me at the helm, our ship wouldn't manage a single night at sea. I'd seen it happen too many times.

My phone rang out from the living room, interrupting my scrubbing of the bathroom countertop, and I dropped the sponge, drying my hands and hurrying toward the sound.

When I reached it and saw the name on the screen, I was tempted to turn back around.

Instead, I found myself lifting the phone to my ear and forcing a cheerful voice. "Hey, Mom."

"Hello," she said, her tone crisp. "Have you talked to your *father?*" She drew out the word.

Fine, thanks. How are you?

"Um, no. No, I haven't. Should I have?"

She huffed dramatically as I picked at a piece of lint on top of the sofa. "Well, I've been trying to call him to check in about how we're going to do Dylan's birthday next month. But I haven't heard back in a few days."

"Do you think something's wrong?"

Another dramatic sigh. "No, I think he's probably in Cabo with Jessica, or Costa Maya with Eleanor, or L.A. with Naomi, or somewhere else with a floozy whose eyelashes are bigger than her brain—"

"I get it," I said, cutting her off. Though it had been my mother's affair that ended their marriage, it was my father who seemed to have made the most of their divorce—a point of contention with my mother. "Do you want me to call him?"

"No, no... There's no sense in that. If he can't be bothered to check up on his family, then we can't force him to." She drew in a long inhale. "It's up to you and me, like always." She clicked her tongue, dragging her sentences out longer and longer. "Always up to us..."

I had to stop myself from rolling my eyes. "Well, Mom, I think Dylan just wants to do something quiet. If you want to come over for dinner and cake, that's fine, but we're not planning anything big this year. He mentioned bringing his new girlfriend over..."

"Girlfriend?" she squealed. "That's when it starts, isn't it? Are they having sex yet? The last thing he needs is a teenage pregnancy when he's got such a bright future—"

"Mom, please," I cut her off again. "I've got it all under control, okay?"

"Are you sure? I know how you get with these things…"

"What things?" I demanded.

"Well, you just really don't know how to handle men who aren't perfect. You got lucky with Peter. He's so calm. So tame. But those boys…what if they take after *your* father, rather than *theirs*? You can't just let them do whatever they want, Ainsley. You have to be on top of things. Testing, talks… Have you thought about having them see a counselor? Are you providing them with condoms? Have you talked to their doctors about HPV vaccinations?"

I recalled the mandatory monthly visits to the doctor from the time I'd started my period as a child. At my mother's insistence, I was tested for STDs constantly, long before I was having sex.

Though I tried to tell her that, she never believed me.

Never believed *in* me.

No matter what I was doing or what I said, she'd never trusted me. I wouldn't do that to my kids. I wanted a better relationship with them than that.

"They're fine. We've had the talk with Dylan, okay? I don't need you to lecture me on—"

"Lecture you? *This* is lecturing? I was under the impression I was just checking up on my daughter. That's your problem, Ainsley. You're so defensive. It's a wonder it hasn't scared Peter off, honestly. You need to loosen up."

"How did we even get on this subject?" I groaned. "We're doing Dylan's birthday dinner at home this year.

33

You can come if you want. I'll make his favorite food, and I'll order him a cake. You don't need to do anything but show up."

"Well, alright. Excuse me for thinking I might be useful. Did you invite your father already?"

"I haven't talked to him, I told you."

"Good." She was quiet for a moment. "It'd be better if you separated the two of us. Maybe he could come over on a different day. Not that he'll come anyway."

"I don't know if he will or not. I can let you know."

"Yes, do that. If he's coming, I'll come on a different day. You'll explain that to Dylan, won't you? It's just too hard."

"I thought you just said you were trying to plan something with him?"

"Well, obviously, he has no interest in doing that with me. And he'll probably end up bringing a date."

I closed my eyes, trying to remain composed. If anyone could cause me to lose control of my rage, it was my mother. "Why don't you bring a date, then?"

She scoffed. "Do you know what it's like for women our age to date?"

Our age? I ran a finger across my lips.

"I'm telling you," she went on, "hold on to Peter, Ainsley. The world isn't kind to divorced women. You hold on to what you've got." I heard her take a sip of something and glanced at the clock. It hadn't yet hit noon, and already she'd been drinking. But I couldn't control her anymore. I needed to focus on what I could still control. "Did you get that email I forwarded you about the new gym in your area? That photo you posted on Facebook

34

looked like you might've gained a little weight. I'm sure Peter wants you to keep yourself up. I was looking into Botox for you, too. I've been getting it personally, and it's a night and day difference for those little crow's-feet you've got around your eyes. Do you want me to send over my girl's information? She charges—"

"Mom," I cut her off, my chest tight. "Thank you, but no. I'm okay. Peter and I are fine. Our kids are fine. My weight and wrinkles are fine. Everything's fine. I promise. You should get yourself out. Join a yoga class or a book club..."

She took another drink. "Yeah, maybe I'll do that. Your father would like that, wouldn't he? He's not the only one who can move on, is he? Hmph." She took a deep, excited breath. "You know what? Maybe we could do a yoga class together? I know this great little place. Tina was telling me all about it—"

"Mom, I'm sorry. I've gotta go. Maisy's home sick, and she needs me." I glanced toward the hall, toward the still silent bedroom. If I had to stay in this conversation for another second, I wasn't sure I'd survive it.

"Sick? Oh, heavens. Is she okay?"

I cringed, picturing the ambulance showing up at my door after I'd broken the news. "She's fine. It's just a stomach bug. Very minor. I'll talk to you later, okay?"

"Okay, let me know if you hear from your father."

"I will."

"And don't tell him I'm asking."

"I won't."

"Tell him I joined a yoga class. Tell him I'm looking better than ever."

"Bye, Mom." I ended the call without waiting for a response, sinking down onto the sofa with a sigh. I should get back to cleaning, but I could feel a headache coming on.

My parents' weird relationship had always been a major stressor all my life, but somehow, I'd imagined it would get better as I got older. Once I had a family of my own. Instead, they'd gotten a messy divorce, and it had just gotten...weirder?

The two were constantly trying to outdo each other.

It seemed miserable and exhausting.

I thought back to the early days, when the news of my mother's affair had gotten out. I'd been sixteen, and none of it made sense to me. It was shortly after that when I'd met him.

The boy I thought would provide me with a means of escaping my family.

The first boy I'd ever loved.

I shook him from my head. Lately, I'd been thinking about him more and more, and I had no idea why.

I pushed myself up from the couch, moving back to the kitchen to finish cleaning, turning on a podcast to keep my mind occupied.

I had enough on my mind.

I had no desire to relive that time—the darkness, the pain. It was over, and I'd moved on.

CHAPTER SIX

PETER

The voice of my assistant, Melodie, came over the speaker of my office phone, startling me.

"Mr. Greenburg, you have someone here to see you. Can I send him back?"

I placed the sandwich back down on the paper it had been wrapped in, dusting off my shirt as I hurriedly chewed the bite of food in my mouth.

"Who is it?" I asked.

"Um, he says his name is Slater," she said cautiously.

My stomach tightened, and I shoved my lunch into the drawer. "Yeah, send him in." I'd nearly forgotten about his missed call the night before. Why had he shown up to the office? I checked my calendar as I waited, a thin sheen of sweat gathering at my brow.

Moments later, I heard two knocks on my door, and it opened before I'd had a chance to welcome him inside.

"Jim," I said, holding out a hand to shake his. "It's been too long, man."

I spied the silver-capped tooth in his mouth as he

grinned, a ball cap over his blond, buzz-cut hair. "Tell me about it." He took a seat in front of my desk without an invitation, and I sat once again. "Hey, I tried to call you last night. You didn't call me back…"

"You did?" I feigned ignorance. "Shoot, sorry. My daughter's sick, and I've been all over the place. Is everything okay? Are we still on schedule with the Cameron project?" Jim never came to my office, but that wasn't the only reason for the uneasy feeling in my chest. He was one of the best contractors on my team, but wherever Jim Slater went, trouble usually followed. Whatever he wanted, I had a feeling it wouldn't be good.

"Yeah, yeah, it's all good. I just need a favor." He grasped his fist with his free hand, leaning back casually in his seat.

"S-sure. What is it?" My own hands balled into fists without volition.

He chuckled. "Don't look so worried. It's no big deal. I just need somewhere to stash a few things for a week or two."

I tried to think. "Okay… You mean here at the office?"

"Nah, I was thinking in that room of yours."

My stomach plummeted, my skin ice cold. We hadn't spoken about the room since the day he finished building it.

"I don't know, man. I don't really let anyone in there."

He looked away, nodding stoically. "Well, I'm not just *anyone*, am I?"

"You know what I mean. What is it you're needing to store?"

His gaze fell to me again, his grin cocky. "It's better if

38

you don't know, trust me. Just let me put a few things in there for a week or two, until things settle down. I'll bring them by tonight." He started to stand, but I reached out a hand.

"What? No! I already said you can't. Maybe I could help you rent a storage unit or something—"

He waved off the suggestion. "Nah, your room is safer."

"Look, Jim, you know I'd do anything to help you, but I can't have anything going on with that room right now—"

"Because the cops are still sniffing around?" he asked, his eyes narrowing.

"Wh-what are you talking about?"

"Ah, Peter, Peter, Peter..." He cracked his knuckles, sounding too much like a mob boss for my taste. He sucked air from behind bared teeth. "See, a few months ago, the cops came around asking questions about you. Apparently, they were following up on a missing persons case about a cop and his wife. Steven something..."

He had the name wrong, but I was too panicked to correct him. I knew the police had approached Beckman and Gina, and a few others around the office, to ask about me—much to my mortification—but I had no idea they'd reached out to our contractors, or anyone else outside of the office when Stefan and Illiana disappeared. They were covering all their bases, I knew, but that didn't stop the experience from being awful.

"So?"

He went on. "So, they asked whether I thought you might've had anything to do with their disappearance, and I guess I could've mentioned the secret room we built for you to hide the bodies of your—"

"*Shut up,*" I whispered hurriedly, already out of my seat and leaning across the desk.

"What? I shouldn't talk about your lair?" He pointed to the sign behind my desk. "Or should I say *Lae Haer?*" He winked. "Nice touch, by the way. I almost didn't catch it."

"Jim, please…"

"Anyway, I heard on the news a few months later that they think he's a rapist." His brows shot up. "I guess you just never know about some people, hm?" His smile changed from playful and carefree to cruel and threatening in a matter of seconds.

"What are you doing? We swore we'd never tell anyone about…any of that."

"Well, terms have changed," he said with a shrug. "You know how it is."

"What do you want?" My jaw was tight. Why had I ever trusted him? I'd known, even then, that it was a mistake. But I never thought he'd betray me. We held each other's secrets, after all.

"To use the room. Like I told you."

I sank back down in my chair. "For a few weeks?"

His head bounced from side to side, his chin wrinkling with an unbothered expression. "Maybe a month."

"Jim, come on, what are you going to do? Rat me out? Honestly?"

"What's the big deal? It's a big enough room. I just need a corner. You do your thing. I won't get in your way."

"You can't come and go in the room. I have a wife.

Kids." I didn't mention that Ainsley knew about the room now. That didn't matter. "I have to be discreet."

He sucked his teeth. "If there's one thing I know, it's how to be discreet. You remember that well, don't you?"

Chills ran over my arms. "Whatever. Fine. A few weeks. A month at most. Come over around midnight, once the kids are in bed, and I'll store your stuff."

He slapped the desk. "Attaboy. I knew you'd come around." With that, he stood, running his fingers down the brim of his cap with a salute. "See you around, Peter."

As he shut the door, dread filled me once again.

A favor was never just a favor with Jim.

I'd learned that the hard way once.

CHAPTER SEVEN

AINSLEY

"So, I had an idea today..."

We were sitting around the dinner table, bowls of soup steaming in front of us. Peter had been distant since he arrived home from work, but I hadn't pressed the issue.

Whatever was bothering him, it would have to wait.

"What idea?" Dylan asked with a scowl.

"Well..." I picked up my spoon, then laid it back down nervously. "I was thinking it would be fun for all of us to go to the lake house next weekend."

Peter's eyes darted up to meet mine. Maisy munched timidly on a cracker, her stomach still queasy. For a moment, no one said a word.

Then, Riley said, "Why?"

I'd expected resistance. The lake house was more of a small cottage we'd bought several years earlier, splitting the cost with Seth and Glennon. It was small and outdated and in an area with not much cell phone service, but it had been a nice reprieve when we'd needed a break and couldn't swing enough time off to take a proper vacation.

Now the house sat empty, mostly. We hadn't been in over a year and Seth and Glennon hadn't in even longer. Once, we'd talked about selling it, but that had been put off.

Now, I was grateful for that. I longed for the quiet evenings in the lake house, curled up in front of the fire, playing board games and making shadow puppets with the kids. Those days were long gone, I knew, but perhaps we could recreate them in some way.

"Well, I thought it might be nice to go before summer ends. You'll all start back to school in just a few weeks, and we haven't done anything during the break. We could grill out, just the five of us. Make s'mores and watch movies. It could be fun." I watched them closely, trying to get a read on what they were thinking.

It was Maisy who spoke up first. "I'm supposed to be going to the movies with Bailey next weekend."

"Yeah," Dylan said, "and I have plans with Julie."

"Plans?" Peter asked. "What plans?"

"We're going to hang out," Dylan said stiffly, picking at the food on his plate.

"I don't have any plans," Riley said—my saving grace. "I think it sounds fun, Mom." He smiled up at me proudly, and I had to wonder what it was he wanted, but I didn't want to push the issue.

"Yeah?" I grinned at him. "Good! Riley's in, who else? Maise, can't you reschedule your movie plans? Go a different day?"

She twisted her mouth in contemplation. "We haven't

43

bought the tickets yet... Can she come to the lake with us, at least?"

I looked at Peter. "Well, I suppose—"

"Yeah! And can Julie come, too?" Dylan asked.

"No," Peter and I said at once.

"That's not fair!" he whined.

"We haven't said anyone can come," Peter reasoned. "But you knew we weren't going to agree to that."

"She can stay in a different room! Come on, Dad, please?"

"Well, if Maisy and Dylan are having friends over, I want to bring someone, too!" Riley chimed in.

"No," I said, cutting off the conversation sharply. "No. No one's coming. No one's bringing anyone. We're going for family time. The five of us. That's it."

Groans were heard all around, but I took another bite of my soup, ignoring them.

"Come on, guys," Peter said halfheartedly. "It'll be fun."

"Whatever," Dylan groaned.

"Fine," Maisy said.

"I guess," Riley grumbled.

"Sounds good, babe," Peter added, though he couldn't hide the worried grin on his face.

I picked up my spoon again, wondering why I'd even bothered. Some part of me still longed for the family we'd once been. Before the secrets and lies. Before the kids grew up.

But we were no longer those people. I was no longer that woman.

The man across from me was no longer that man.

Could I bring them back? Or had too much changed after all?

If I gave up on them, what did that mean for our futures?

CHAPTER EIGHT

PETER

Despite years of sharing a bed with her, I'd never gotten used to how peaceful my wife looked while she was sleeping. Perhaps it was because I never saw her in such a state while she was awake.

It always amazed me, the sheer quietness of her face— no expression, no stress lines. She was just...existing.

I watched her breathing, her chest rising and falling steadily, as I waited for the text to come from Jim to let me know he was pulling down the driveway.

I had to hope Ainsley would stay asleep through it all, that I'd be able to sneak whatever this was into the room without her noticing.

Maybe I should've just told her what was happening, but I knew my wife. I knew she wouldn't have been okay with the blackmail—because that's what it was at the end of the day.

I was being blackmailed by a man I once considered my best friend.

Of course, that was before I knew who he was. Before I knew what he'd done.

Before he brought me into his world and ruined my life.

I'd met Jim the week I moved into my college dorm. As my roommate, he was my default friend, and because I had no others, I latched on to him.

I'd never had a good relationship with the men in my life—my dad and older brothers—and I'd had very few friends growing up, so I'm embarrassed to admit how desperately I wanted Jim's approval.

I thought he was cool.

Three years older, despite being a freshman like I was, he was one of those guys with an effortless swagger and confidence I couldn't have attempted if I was paid to.

I still have no idea why he let me hang around him back then—maybe more for amusement than anything—but I was so glad he did. I did whatever he asked: wrote his essays, paid for his books, cleaned his side of the dorm.

Anything.

Everything.

Whatever it took to fit in with him.

And in the end, *everything* was exactly what it took.

I wasn't supposed to be in the dorm that night. I should've been home for fall break, but my parents had been fighting and all I could think about was how badly I wanted to get back to school.

It was the only place I felt safe.

The only place I didn't feel five years old anymore.

When I walked into our dorm to see the two naked bodies on our floor—Jim on top of a girl I didn't recognize—I panicked. I'd accidentally seen him having sex before, but it was something we'd mitigated with a sock on the door.

This time, because he wasn't expecting me, there was no sock.

"Sorry," I'd said, covering my eyes and trying to shuffle out of the room quickly.

He hadn't responded and I'd slammed the door, feeling useless. I wasn't wanted at home, my parents probably hadn't even noticed I'd left, and now I wasn't welcome there. I had nowhere to go. Nothing to do.

I walked across the dark quad, feeling miserable and alone, and found an empty bench to sit down on for a while. An hour later, my phone buzzed in my pocket and I pulled it out, spying Jim's number on my screen.

Was he angry?

Would he yell at me?

Would he laugh it off?

Tease me about wanting to sneak a peek?

I could never tell.

I opened my phone and pressed it to my ear. "Yeah?"

"You can come back now."

I tried to get a read on his tone, but I couldn't.

"You sure? No rush on my end."

"Yeah," he said simply. "We're done." Before I could say anything else, he'd ended the call. I slid it back into my pocket and stood, taking my time as I made my way back to our dorm.

But when I reached it and opened the door, a joke ready on my lips, my smile fell away immediately. Jim was dressed and on the bed, but the girl was still on our floor, still not dressed. It didn't take long for me to realize she was unconscious.

Or...dead?

No, her chest rose with a shallow breath.

"What the hell, man?" I demanded, pointing to her. Why was he just sitting there? Why didn't he look worried? I kneeled down next to her, touching her face and trying to ignore her bare body, no matter how hard it was. "Is she okay?"

"Not really," he said simply, standing from the bed.

"What do you mean?" A chill ran over me as he moved to stand behind me.

"You want a turn?" he asked, laughing dryly.

"What do you mean?" I asked again, feeling vomit rising in my chest.

He leaned down, gripping the back of my neck tight with one hand. "I said, do you want a turn?"

I jerked out of his grasp. "What the fuck are you talking about? What's wrong with her?"

"Not a thing," he said, adjusting his pants. "Trust me." I was going to be sick. "See for yourself."

"She's not waking up."

"Exactly. She won't know the difference, kid."

"Is she drunk?"

"What the fuck are you asking questions for?" he asked, angry then. His hand was back on my neck, his grip tighter. "I thought we were cool, Greenburg."

"We *are* cool," I said, staring down at her again. I couldn't bring myself to move. I'd heard about it, of course. Date raping women. I'd seen the drugs passed around campus, but I had no idea Jim was into that sort of thing.

He was so cool.

He slept with plenty of women.

I couldn't imagine why he'd need to do this.

"So, then, be cool. I'm offering you a gift. Not many friends I'd let have a girl when I'm done with her."

I didn't want to do it—it felt awkward. Wrong too, I guess, but my main concern was of trying to have sex in front of someone. Jim, especially. I worried he'd make fun of me.

"You gonna do it or no?"

"I'm... I'm okay." I started to stand up, but he placed a hand on my shoulder, stopping me.

"Nah, you're not. 'Cause the way I see it, you're either gonna fuck her or you're gonna snitch."

"I won't snitch," I swore. "You know me better than that."

"Then you know your other option, don't ya? Look, it ain't about knowin' ya, kid. You gotta prove it." He lifted his foot to her leg, nudging her forcefully with his toes. "See? She's not waking up." He paused. "And when you're done, you can do me a favor and help me get rid of her."

Something about the way he'd said those words, the look in his eye, said he'd get rid of me, too, if I didn't do exactly as he'd said. And so, I did.

No more arguing.

I proved it.

I tried not to think about him watching me as I did it.

When it was over, we dressed her and took her to the

woods. Jim told me to leave him there with her and I'd never been so grateful to get away.

I remembered watching him get back in the truck after what felt like a lifetime later. He was calm. Surprisingly calm. He put the truck into drive without a word. It was then that I noticed the blood on his hands. It was dark, so I couldn't be sure that was what it was, but somehow, I knew.

I didn't know she was going to die.

Not really.

I don't know what I thought about why he wanted to be alone with her, or what he'd meant by *get rid of her,* but that wasn't it. The rest of the ride back to our dorm was filled with silence. I felt sick to my stomach. Terrified of my roommate.

When we finally parked, he turned to look at me with a wicked grin and said something I've never forgotten.

"There's nothing like it, Greenburg. Watchin' 'em go. Watchin' the lights go out. You're their god in that moment. It's a high unlike any other."

I don't remember if I said anything then…

Maybe I just stared at him. Maybe I nodded.

All I remember is the way he stared at me. The way he smelled—of blood and sweat and sex.

The way I knew everything was going to change.

From that night on, I didn't ask any questions. I did everything he told me to because I was terrified, but eventually, because it became fun, just like he said it would.

I liked the power that came with it. Liked knowing I was in control of everything.

Finally, I understood the confidence Jim had. Maybe

some of it had even rubbed off on me, too.

Meeting Jim Slater was the best and worst thing that had ever happened to me and, even now, I wasn't sure I could honestly say I would change a thing. I wanted to be the kind of person who would take it all back, given the chance, but I wasn't. Try as I might, I couldn't lie to myself about that.

My phone buzzed in my palm, bringing me back to the present. I glanced down at the screen, reading over the short text, and sliding from the bed.

I eased out of the room carefully, down the hall, then down the stairs and toward the garage. I snuck out the side door, cautious not to let it slam as I jogged toward the driveway where I could see the gray truck coming to a stop.

"Sup?" he said, when the door opened. As usual, he was casual and carefree. As if we weren't meeting up in the middle of the night to stash *god knows what* in my secret murder room.

"Did you bring it?"

"Yep." He slammed the driver's door shut and moved around to the back, rubbing his hands together as if he were cold.

"Shh," I warned. "Keep it down. Please. I don't want my wife or kids to hear us."

He looked up at me, a sly grin on his lips. "They've got you on a tight leash, don't they, Greenburg?"

"It's not like that."

He chuckled, but didn't look convinced. "If you say so. Seems like someone needs to be put in their place." His wink caused my stomach to churn.

At the back of the truck, he tossed back a black tarp.

"What is it you're wanting me to keep for you anyway?"

"Like I told you, it's better if you don't know." He may as well have patted me on the head. With a sharp tug, he pulled out a large duffel bag, tossing it over one shoulder and walking toward the garage without needing directions.

It had probably been a mistake to let Jim build the room in the first place, truth be told. I knew that when I'd done it. But there was no one else I'd trust to build it. I needed someone who wouldn't ask too many questions, who'd make sure not to mention it to Ainsley or anyone else. Jim was the guy for the job, as much as I'd hated it. I had to make sure my family was protected from my secrets, even if it meant relying on a man I wasn't sure I could rely on at all.

When Beckman and I started the firm—Beckman providing the capital and my expertise providing the framework—it had been a no-brainer to bring Jim on. He ran one of the biggest contracting firms in the city, and I knew he'd be a great partner. Despite his flaws, Jim knew how to get things done. He made friends with everyone and could always get a discount or adjust a timeline without issue. I worried I'd made a deal with the devil back then, but truth be told, our partnership had been completely cordial.

When Ainsley and I'd gotten married and I stepped out of all the habits Jim had taught me, he'd accepted it without qualms. He trusted me by then, as much as he'd ever trusted anyone. Though I still had reservations about being involved with him, even professionally, I'd thought it was better to keep him close.

Now, I had to wonder how long he'd been waiting to hold what he knew about my past over my head. Maybe that was all he was ever trying to do—gather as much dirt on everyone around him as he could. To control them. To control everything.

Was this all happening because he needed a place to store something? Or was this the perfect opportunity to draw me back into his world?

Honestly, I was scared to find out.

He pushed open the door and we walked toward the wall. When we'd reached it, he stepped back, allowing me to shove the shelf down a smidge and press the bricks that would open the hidden door.

When it opened, I smelled the familiar, musty scent. It had been too long since I'd been in the room. Something about it set my skin on fire, my body tingling with excitement.

When Jim walked into it, the excitement disappeared.

It felt wrong to have him there.

In the space I'd reserved only for myself and the most special of my victims.

He looked around, letting out a whistle. "I forgot how nice this place was."

"You can put that over here," I said, pointing to the corner farthest from where I'd once hidden my bag. The left side of the room was mostly bare, just a small tarp wadded up in the corner, a hose, and the drain.

He placed the bag on the ground next to the tarp, looking around with a long, drawn-out inhale.

"How long do you need me to keep it?"

"A few days," he said. "A week, maybe two. I'll let you know when I'm ready to pick it up."

"And you're not going to tell me what's in it?" I could always just open it when he left.

"Nope. And I'd suggest you don't look in it." He stalked past me, then turned around and stared in my direction, his face cloaked in shadows. "Curiosity killed the cat, 'n all."

I nodded. "I won't touch it. Just...let me know when you're ready for it."

"Will do." He pulled the truck keys from his pocket and twirled them around his finger, still not moving.

"And you're going to keep all of this quiet, right?"

"All this?" He seemed confused. "The room, you mean?"

"Mhm."

"Relax, Peter. Your secrets have always been safe with me." His hand gripped my shoulder suddenly, making me flinch. "You scratch my back, I'll scratch yours." His eyes drilled into mine, my skin crawling. "Same as before."

Suddenly, I was flashing back to that night.

Stupid.

Vulnerable.

Weak.

With Jim, I'd always be the Peter from that night.

Visions flashed through my head—the blood, the woods where we'd buried her, the way he'd laughed afterward.

I was terrified, but also intrigued...

I'd wanted to be him.

In some sick way, I guess I still did.

"We should probably go. I don't want Ainsley to wake up."

He released my shoulder with a stiff nod. "Understood." With that, he backed away slowly, the sole of his boot sliding against the concrete floor.

Once we'd made it out of the room and I'd secured it closed, he crossed the garage, reaching for the door with one final wave over his head. "Thanks again, Greenburg."

"You bet," I said, as if this were an everyday favor.

When he shut the door, I waited silently, listening for the truck to start up. Once it had, once I'd heard it backing down the long drive, I breathed a sigh of relief.

There. That's done.

When I opened the door to go back inside, Ainsley was standing in the hallway, her arms crossed in front of her chest. My body tensed as I tried to come up with a lie.

How long had she been standing there?

What had she heard?

What had she seen?

What did she know?

"Hey," I said. "Sorry, did I wake you?"

"What were you doing?"

"I, um, sorry..." I scratched the back of my neck.

Lie.

Lie better than this, Peter.

"One of our contractors is heading out of town for a project, and I had to give him a few forms before he left."

"Why didn't you just email them?"

She didn't believe me. I didn't blame her.

"He's old school. Still uses a flip phone. But, seriously,

one of the best." I moved to walk past her, hoping to end the line of questioning, but she wasn't done. I knew she wasn't even before she spoke again.

"Why did he come by in the middle of the night, then? Why not this evening? Why didn't you tell me he was coming? We said no more lies, no more secrets, and—"

I cut her off, gripping her shoulders gently. "Ains, breathe. No more secrets. I'm not lying. I had no idea he was coming. I woke up because my phone was buzzing and he asked me for the forms. He was supposed to come by in the morning, but he decided to head out late tonight instead. I didn't tell you because I didn't think it was a big enough deal to wake you up about."

She stared at me skeptically, so I leaned forward, pressing my lips to hers. "Want me to prove it? I'll call him if you want me to."

As much as Ainsley knew me, there were a few things I knew well about her. Well enough to bet my life on. Like the fact that she'd never admit to anyone else—well, anyone aside from Glennon—that we had issues or that she felt she couldn't trust me.

"No, it's fine," she said with a huff, pulling out of my arms and walking back to our bedroom without another word.

I didn't want to lie to her anymore, but I had no choice. This was Jim's fault. I was trying to be who she wanted, but I had to do this to protect her. To protect us all.

Once the favor was done, things would go back to normal.

No, they'd go forward to being perfect.

CHAPTER NINE

AINSLEY

H e was lying, again, but I didn't know why.

All I knew was that there was still something keeping us apart. I loved my husband, but how much longer could we go on like this?

How much longer could we pretend things were okay?

As I slid back into bed, my body radiated with anger, but I couldn't allow it to consume me. Something had to change, and I'd be the one to change it.

I rolled over to face him, running my hand across his chest. He looked shocked, then pleased, the redness fading from his cheeks.

"Do you miss it?" I asked, working to keep my expression unchanged.

His eyes narrowed. "Miss what?"

I glanced down, then back up. "*It.*"

"It?" He was playing dumb, but I was game.

"What you did in that room."

His Adam's apple bobbed, his face blanching. I felt his heart begin to race under my palm.

"No," he said after a moment's pause. "Of course I don't. Why would you ask me that?"

"You told me it was an addiction. After you found my note. The night it all came out. You said it was like an addiction… Now you've given it up cold turkey. You must miss it."

He looked away from me, pulling the cover up over his chest farther. "Why are we even talking about this?"

"Because we can."

"Well, we shouldn't."

"Says who?" I challenged.

"Says me, Ainsley. What the hell are you trying to do? Start a fight?"

"*No*," I said gently. "I'm not trying to start a fight or trick you. Of course I'm not. I just want to understand it —*you*—better."

He snorted. "I think you understand me well enough."

He had a point. "But not that part of you. Not the you who exists in that room."

"You don't want to know that version of me." He still wouldn't meet my eyes.

I gripped his chin, turning his face to look at me. "Peter, please…"

He resisted my pull, but eventually gave in. His face was red again, not from lying, but from pure shame. "What?" I heard the exasperation in his voice. "What do you want from me, Ainsley? You know what I've done. I haven't done anything, haven't hurt anyone since that night. Since Illiana. What do you want me to say?"

I sat up, leaning against the headboard. "I want you to tell me about it."

59

"What about it?"

"Everything. What does it feel like? Who are you in that room? I want you to tell me everything."

"Why?" He winced, shaking his head. "Why would you want that? I'm a monster, remember?"

"You're not a monster," I argued, feeling embarrassed by my lashing out that night. "I shouldn't have said that. I was angry."

"You were right to call me that. It's…accurate."

"It can't be. I know you, Peter." I didn't believe it. Maybe some small part of him had monsterlike qualities, but more important than that, there was a man I loved sitting in front of me. A broken man. A man I could fix if I could just understand where the break was.

"You know a version of me. You don't know what it's like in there. What I'm like."

"So tell me." I just needed to get him talking. If I could get him to open up, I was sure we'd be able to get to the root of it all. What made him tick? What brought out the monster?

"I can't," he said, his voice cracking. He hated himself, and I couldn't blame him, but he needed me to make this right. Somehow, I had to believe I could.

I gripped his arm, pleading with him. "Peter, we can't be in this together if you won't tell me the truth about everything. This is what's driving us apart. This is what's always driven us apart, even before I knew what it was. You keep this wall up between us in order to protect me from the truth, but I've known the truth for years and I'm still here. Can't you understand that?"

He was silent for a moment, then pulled the covers off his legs and sat up, his back to me.

"What are you do—"

"No," he cut me off.

"Wha—"

"No. I can't understand that."

"Peter—"

He scowled, looking over his shoulder at me for a second. He was staring at me as if I disgusted him. "You're perfect, okay? You're perfect and put together, and you never lose control of yourself, you never break down. You never lose your cool. I'm not like you."

"That... That's not entirely true. And, even if it was, I never expected you to be like me." I liked knowing that was how he saw me, despite it being untrue. "I want you to be like you."

"But you can't understand it. Even if I tell you what it's like, unless you've lived it, you can't understand what it's like. You'll just think I'm crazy. You'll realize it's been a mistake to stay with me. It's better to keep you in the dark. To keep you on that side of the wall."

I slid across the bed toward him, placing a hand on his back, but he shied away. "Is that what you think?"

"It's what I know."

I moved to sit next to him, pulling his chin and giving him no choice but to look at me. "Peter, you're wrong. I may seem put together, but it's only because that's what's always been expected of me. I never had any choice but to keep pretending like I'm perfect. Like everything's perfect. My mother put me in a fat camp at age seven. I was seven years old, I barely had any understanding of body image, but already I was told that I wasn't good enough. Normal enough. From there, it was a constant state of worry. She was always fussing over my hair, highlighting it and straightening the slightest frizz. I never felt perfect—not then and not now."

I shook my head. When he didn't reply, I went on. "And the way I coped—bingeing and purging with food, running through my neighborhood every single day until my feet bled and I'd burned off every calorie I'd consumed, pretending to be perfect, pretending I enjoyed it—it wasn't healthy. I've tried my hardest to be the opposite of who my mother is. I don't talk to the kids about their bodies or their appearances. For a long time, I thought the only person I've tried to control was myself. But then, after the Stefan thing, I started to see patterns. I realized then, the things I thought I was fixing, the ways I tried to keep things perfect—that was me controlling you, all without ever even realizing it. I thought I was being kind by keeping things in order. It was my way of showing you I loved you. Showing the kids that I loved them. But it wasn't any better than what my mom did. Not really." I sighed, pinching the bridge of my nose.

"Oh, Ains, that's not true—"

"It is. The truth is, I always thought I would do better than she had. But I haven't." My body revolted against the confession, my skin cold, mouth dry. I'd never allowed myself to admit my darkest fear until that moment.

"You're not your mother." He seemed shocked, his jaw slack. His eyes showed a seriousness that warmed the pit of my stomach. "And you're not controlling. You've done what you had to do. It's because of you that we have such

62

good kids. They're kind, they get good grades, they never get into real trouble. Trust me, they didn't get any of that from me."

"You have a dark side to you, I won't deny that. But you *are* kind. Do you remember...when Dylan was first learning to walk, and you went out and bought all of those padded corner guards and Styrofoam? You had the house coated in them. All to protect him."

"Of course I did. I love our kids."

"You always have. And what about the Christmas gifts you buy for the people at work? Or the way you always stop when we notice someone broken down on the side of the road. There are so many different versions of who you are..." I rubbed my hand across his arm, and this time, he didn't pull away. "And I love each and every one."

His guard had come down, if only by a tiny bit. "I want to be better for you. For the kids. I swear to you I've tried. It's just...sometimes I lose control. I've...it's like..." He held his hands out, palms up, fingers bent like claws as if he were trying to grip the thought from thin air. Finally, he cut himself off, shaking his head.

"Tell me what it's like," I insisted. "Please tell me. I won't judge you...or...or fear you. I just want to under-stand it the best I can."

"How will you ever be able to understand it when I can't even understand it?"

"Maybe I can help with that. And, if we can under-stand why you do it, maybe we can find a way to..." I didn't want to say *fix you*, which was the phrase on the tip of my tongue. Though it was my nature to fix everything in our life, maybe the solution to this problem was just letting things happen as they would. To fight against my very nature, as painful as it was, just as I was asking Peter to fight against his. "To make things easier for you."

"Easier how?" He seemed intrigued.

"I don't know until you tell me what you know. What you do. Tell me everything and let me help you work through it all. No judgment. No fighting."

He groaned, hanging his head. "You don't know what you're asking me."

"I do. I know it's a lot, but I need you to trust me." He met my eyes warily. "Like I'm trusting you."

He seemed to be contemplating, then huffed in a big breath as if preparing to head into battle. "Okay, well, don't say I didn't warn you."

"I won't."

He ran a palm over his face. "Well, you... I mean, you know the gist of it. I...I lose control. It can be the smallest thing that sets me off, and suddenly, I can't stop it. I can't help myself. The only thing that makes me feel better... that makes me feel like I have any control, any power—"

"So, it's about power for you? Not attraction?"

I heard the scowl in his voice before it appeared on his face, as if it were the most ridiculous suggestion in the world. "Yes. God, yes, Ains. It's never been about attraction. I only want to...to feel powerful." He shook his head. "I sound ridiculous. I can't explain it."

"So it makes you feel powerful, then? Good? Does it make you feel...feel *good?*"

He hesitated, his eyes dancing between mine as if contemplating denying it, but already I could see the light in his expression.

He was remembering.

He'd left me for the moment, stepped back into a piece of his life I wasn't a part of.

I needed to bring him back. "You can be honest. I need you to be honest."

"It's the best feeling in the world." He didn't break eye contact with me, in a split second of pure vulnerability, and I knew the way I handled this would be the determining factor in where our conversation went. I needed him to trust me, above all else. I couldn't focus on my own conflicting emotions; Peter was all that mattered.

"Okay. Tell me more…"

His expression changed again, the vulnerability washing away, his eyes burning dark. "It's…it's like… In that room, in that moment, I'm the whole world. I'm the whole world, Ains. I control everything. Whether they live. Whether they die. I'm the only one who gets to control any of it. In the beginning, they beg me to give them mercy, but by the end…they're begging for death." As if he hadn't meant to say it, the dark desire in his eyes disappeared for half a second, gauging my reaction, but when I didn't budge, it returned. "It's the only thing that makes me feel like I have any control in this world, Ainsley. We go through so much of our lives being controlled by others—our jobs, the government, our parents—" He didn't say *our wives,* but somehow I knew it was next on the list. My fingers tensed in my lap, though he didn't seem to notice. He'd let me in, finally. I couldn't ruin that. "And so much is uncontrollable anyway. *Everything* is uncontrollable, really. Except this. With this, I'm in complete control. It's exhilarating. Like the only time I get to feel alive. It's hard to explain to someone who hasn't experienced it." He glanced down at the bedspread, seeming to realize where he was. His face clouded with uneasiness.

I needed to say something. Anything. "I know what you mean."

His eyes bounced back up in shock. "What?"

"I may not know exactly how it feels, but I do understand what you're saying. That night with Stefan, once I'd gotten over the terror of it all, it was invigorating. In the worst and best way."

"But it's different...actually doing the killing."

"I may not have swung the bat, Peter, but I brought him here and practically handed it to you."

He pressed his lips together but didn't argue, though I could see he wanted to. I didn't force the issue.

"Knowing you'd seen me for what I was that night, knowing you'd seen me cross that line, worrying you'd seen me enjoying it... It was the most terrified I've ever felt."

I flinched as he said the words. "Do you...do you miss it?"

He was quiet for a second, then pushed himself off the bed and walked across the room, away from me. For a moment, I thought he was going to leave, but instead, he sat down at my vanity, staring at himself in the mirror.

"Peter?"

"I miss it every single day. I have to fight against it, actively stop myself from thinking about it... Every time I have a bad day at work, or we get into a fight, or my parents or brothers drive me crazy, literally all I want to do is find someone and kill them. Destroy them. It's the only thing that brings me clarity."

I was silent, letting what he'd said wash over me. For a long time, I'd known what my husband did. I'd known his darkness.

But knowing it and hearing it from him firsthand were two different things. As much as I'd told myself I could be okay with everything, I found myself conflicted. I was a woman, after all. I was raising a daughter. It was men like him that made life harder for us all. Terrifying for us all. But that didn't stop me from loving him. It didn't make me want him less. I just had to find a way to prove that to him.

"Well?" he asked when I didn't immediately respond.

My eyes flicked up to meet his in the mirror. "You were right. You are a monster." His shoulders fell, and I stood up from the bed, moving toward him. I crossed the room, reaching him at the vanity and touching his shoulder gently.

When he turned to look at me, I wanted to wash the shame from his broken expression. I wanted him to see how much I still loved him. That our love was all that mattered.

"But you're *my* monster. And as long as you're completely honest with me, I'm not going anywhere."

CHAPTER TEN

PETER

A few days later, I'd just stepped out of the office when my phone began to buzz in my pocket. My mind flashed to Ainsley and the kids, wondering which of them it might be and what might be wrong, but those worries were quickly replaced when I saw the name on the screen.

Jim.

"Hello?"

"Hey. Where are you right now?"

"Uh, I'm at work…" I glanced across the street at the building that held my office, then back toward the sandwich shop I was standing behind. "Why?"

He sniffed. "Need another small favor."

My jaw tightened instinctually. "What kind of favor?"

"I need to put something else in that room of yours."

"What?" I demanded, keeping my voice low. "No. You said the one bag was all. And you're supposed to only be keeping it there for a few days."

"I know what I said, but plans have changed. Relax, it's

just one more, slightly larger package. I'll have everything out of there before you know it."

I pinched the bridge of my nose, thinking quickly. "Jim, look, I've already told you...I don't want to draw attention to the fact that the room is even there in the first place. I can't have my wife or kids finding it. I only go in that room when absolutely necessary. We can't just keep—"

"It is," he said, cutting me off. "It is *absolutely necessary*, Greenburg. And since I'm doing you a favor and keeping quiet about the room, I thought you'd want to return the favor for me. Was I wrong?"

I heard the thinly veiled threat in his voice. "Come on, man. What are you doing? Are you really going to turn me in?"

"No," he said, letting out a breath. "Of course not." I breathed a sigh of relief. Then he added, "You wouldn't be stupid enough to let it get to that... Would you?"

I shook my head, stepping back as a couple passed me on the sidewalk, still trying to keep my voice low. "Fine. But it's just one more thing, right?"

"One more," he said. "Scout's honor."

"Fine, you can come by tonight."

"No, I need to come now."

"Now? What are you talking about? I'm working. You're supposed to be working. You can't just come by when I'm not home."

"So come home."

"Jim, come on..."

He was silent. Waiting.

"Can't it wait until tonight? I've got three meetings this afternoon."

"So meet me now. It won't take five minutes and you can still make your meetings."

I couldn't. Even if I made it home in thirty minutes—and that was best-case scenario—once we got the package in the room and left, I'd be late for my first meeting with a new client, which would push back the rest of my afternoon, making me late for everything. But what choice did I have?

I glanced at my watch.

"Fine. Half an hour."

"Attaboy," he said proudly. With that, the call ended and I abandoned my lunch plans, zipping back across the street toward the parking garage.

I had to hope this would be the last time Jim would ask for a favor. That this would buy his silence. But if it wasn't, I had to deal with the fact that I could either live like this forever, or take matters into my own hands.

I'd promised Ainsley I wouldn't hurt anyone anymore.

That there would be no more secrets.

But sometimes, our hands are forced.

Sometimes, the secrets don't give you any choice.

When I made it to the house, Jim was already there. His gray truck sat in the driveway. Waiting. Warning of danger.

He stepped from the truck just as I pulled my car to a stop. Once I'd made it out of the vehicle, he circled around to the back of the truck, staring into the bed.

"Thanks for coming," he said casually, as if he hadn't forced me. Every vein, every nerve, every muscle in my body tinged with rage. What was meant to be a smile felt more like a grimace.

"No problem." I was going to control myself. Just like I'd promised Ainsley. I could do it. Really, I could.

Even if I'd already murdered him a thousand ways in my mind.

It was just one more favor. That was it.

He was still standing behind the truck, apparently waiting for me. I stopped several feet away, my brows raised. "Ready?"

"Yeah." He lowered the tailgate. "I'm gonna need your help with this one. It's pretty big."

"How big?"

I walked around the truck, dreading whatever would be inside, and when I saw the *package*, as he'd misleadingly called it, I froze.

Before, the black plastic tarp had been used to cover the boxes in the back of his truck.

This time, it was wrapped around a body.

CHAPTER ELEVEN

AINSLEY

I scanned the park, buzzing with parents and children as I watched for my kids to make an appearance. I was still uneasy with the idea of them spending their afternoons at the park with friends while we were at work—this was only the second summer I'd allowed them to do so—but I was working on giving them each more freedom as long as they earned it. This kind of freedom, this kind of respect, it would've meant the world to me as a child.

Still, that didn't stop me from worriedly searching the crowd for their features when I was supposed to pick them up.

Maisy's wavy brown hair.

Riley's playful smile and thinning frame.

It never got old—seeing them there. Seeing them happy. With their friends. Playing. Searching for me.

It would be my last summer of picking the three of them up together. Next year, Dylan would be driving.

He'd be able to take them and drop them off, as well as bring them home.

It seemed impossible to me, he'd be fifteen next month. Some days, I caught myself thinking of him as the little boy with skinned-up knees and mussy hair.

Although, most days, he still had mussy hair.

It was all going by so fast, and I knew once he turned sixteen, the years would go even faster. How were we down to so few milestones left? So few holidays and birthdays?

We were running out of time all around, and that never failed to take my breath away when I contemplated it.

Where had the time gone?

Even with the time we had left, it seemed like they were too busy to cherish any of it.

I didn't want to take their childhood from them. I wanted them to enjoy it while it lasted, but that didn't mean it didn't sting.

When they were little, I'd once dreamed of the day I'd accept the management position, because it would mean I could set my own schedule—leaving when I needed to in order to pick up the kids or spend time with them. As a teller, and then as a banker, there were so many times they'd needed me to pick them up from school or attend an event, and due to my work schedule, I hadn't been able to.

It was the cruelest irony that now that I could set my own schedule and show up for them when they needed me, they hardly ever needed me.

The phone buzzed and I glanced down at the screen, spying Glennon's name.

"Hello?"

"Hey, love. What are you up to?"

"Oh, just picking up the kids from the park. How's the trip going?"

"Really well," she said, dragging out the words. "It's beautiful out here. Seth was right, these mountains are nothing like what we have back home."

"Well, don't get any funny ideas about packing up and moving to Colorado. I'd miss you too much."

"You don't have to worry about that." The warmth of her voice reminded me of how much I missed her. After their divorce, she and Seth had reconciled almost immediately. It was the most amicable divorce in history, as far as I was concerned. Then again, I guessed when feelings weren't involved, it did make things easier.

From time to time, I found myself longing for Peter and me to learn how they'd managed it.

Now, Glennon and Seth had moved back in together—strictly as best friends and roommates—and as far as I could tell, they hadn't missed a beat.

When I'd expressed concern over the arrangement, worrying it might cause one of them to get hurt, Glennon assured me my fears were unfounded. They'd simply spent so much time together neither of them could bear the thought of being apart.

"Well, good," I said. "Are you at the hotel, then?"

"Not yet. We stopped for a bite to eat before Seth's meeting this evening. We'll check in, in just a few hours. I just wanted to call and see how Maisy's recital went."

"Her recit…" I trailed off, my stomach dropping. How could I have forgotten? I checked the date on my phone.

Yesterday.

Her recital was yesterday, the tenth, same as it had been every year since she was four. She'd been out with Bailey yesterday. Had they gone to the recital without me? Had she been expecting me to be there and I'd missed it? Why hadn't she mentioned it? Why hadn't I caught it? I placed my head on my steering wheel, my body filling with a cold dread.

No wonder she'd hardly spoken to me this morning…

"Glen, I forgot."

"Forgot?" she asked, as shocked as I was.

"I don't know how I could've been so stupid. She was out with friends last night, or at least, that's what I thought, and I just… I don't know. I spaced. What do I do? How do I tell her how sorry I am? She must hate me."

"Okay…" She was the voice of reason carrying across the line, her tone soothing. "Just breathe, okay? She doesn't hate you. She could never hate you. It was an honest mistake. You just need to talk to her. Ask her how it went. Make sure she knows you didn't plan to miss it."

I thought back over the past few months, trying to recall the last time I'd attended a practice with her, but failing.

Once, I'd been there every Thursday night without fail, but when her friends started joining her team, there'd been carpools and changes of plans, and eventually, I'd been traded out for the dance moms whose entire lives revolved around their children's dance careers. Somehow, until that moment, I'd never realized it.

That's how it happens, isn't it?

It's one tiny change of plan. The first time your child doesn't want you to hold them. The last time they ask you to play with them.

Just baby steps and minuscule differences, and we all just assume it's a hiccup…that things will go back to the way things have been if we just keep on trying. Keep believing. Keep assuming things are normal.

But they aren't because there is no normal.

Normal doesn't exist and it never has.

There are just these periods where things feel safe and calm, and then, long before we're ready, everything's torn apart and we call it change.

We look back at our lives and wonder when it all changed, but the truth is…the better question is, when didn't it?

Because we're always changing. Life is always changing.

It's the rarer moments where things are still.

"I've gotta go," I said, spying Maisy's head peering through the crowd. She had one hand over her eyes, shielding them from the sun when she caught sight of me. "She's coming over now."

"It's going to be okay. Promise. Love you."

"Love you," I said, ending the call as Maisy pulled open the door and climbed inside.

I prayed she wouldn't notice the tears in my eyes as I said, "Hey, baby."

Her brows furrowed, caught off guard by the warm, unfamiliar greeting. Her cheeks were bright red from the sun and the heat.

"Um, hey…"

"Where are your brothers?"

"Somewhere." She waved her hand casually over her shoulder, not meeting my eyes. "I told them to come on."

"Maise, I wanted to talk to you…"

"About what?" She'd already pulled out a book from her bag, one by Margaret Peterson Haddix, and opened it to the place she had marked.

"About last night."

"What was last night?" Now I had her attention.

"Your recital," I played along. "Honey, I'm so sorry I forgot about it. I don't have any excuse. It just slipped my mind… You know I would've been there no matter what if I'd remembered. Why didn't you say anything?"

Her brows drew down again, her head cocked to the side, then her expression smoothed, her mouth dropping open. "Oh, no. Mom, it's fine. I didn't have a recital last night."

"You didn't?" Relief filled me, replaced quickly with confusion. "What do you mean? Why didn't you? Did they reschedule it?" To my knowledge, they'd never rescheduled a summer recital.

"No," she said calmly. "I'm sure they had it, I just didn't dance."

"But why not?"

The door to the car opened and Riley climbed inside. I smiled at him, then turned my attention back to Maisy, who still hadn't answered me. "Why didn't you dance?"

"You're dancing again?" Riley asked, buckling himself in with a bag of chips held between his teeth.

Maisy cast a sideways glance at him as I processed what was happening.

"*Again?* What do you mean? Did you stop dancing?"

Riley's cheeks flushed bright red as he looked between us. "She didn't know?"

The door opened again and Dylan climbed inside, oblivious to the tension. He swiped the bag of chips from Riley. "Didn't know what? What's going on?"

"Hey, give those back!" Riley whined, trying to take the chips back from his brother.

"Maisy?" I called over the commotion.

She opened her book, not bothering to look at me. "It's nothing, Mom. Please don't make a big deal about it. I just don't want to dance anymore."

"Since when?"

"Can you turn up the air?" Dylan asked. "It's a million degrees in here."

I wasn't listening. "You can't just stop showing up to practice and recitals, Maise. Your team is counting on you."

"You're dancing again?" Dylan asked, making it clear I was the only one out of the loop.

"No," she told him, then looked at me. "It's fine. I didn't just stop showing up. I told Coach last year I wasn't going to come back. I didn't dance in the fall or spring, either. I thought you knew."

"Why didn't anyone call me? Why didn't you tell me? Does your dad know? Why are we still paying for your lessons?"

"Mom, the air!" Dylan panted, fanning himself.

"You aren't. I never asked for the money after last

summer and neither of you have been taking me to lessons, so I thought you'd gotten the hint. I'm sorry, I wasn't trying to hide it from you. Are you mad?"

I shook my head. How had I missed something so important. I felt two feet tall. "Of course I'm not mad, sweetheart. Of course not. I'm...surprised. I thought you loved dance."

Tired of waiting for me, Dylan unbuckled, leaning past me and cranking the air up to full blast.

"I did love it, I guess. But I'm not into it anymore."

I turned the air down a bit, trying to hear her better. "Why not? What about your friends? Are they still doing it?"

"No, we all quit. Bailey quit in the middle of the season last year, but Jennessa and I stuck it out until the recital."

I shook my head, huffing out a breath. How had I missed so much? Why hadn't anyone told me? How many times had I talked to her friends' parents and no one mentioned it to me? Why? Did they think I knew? Were they trying to hide it from me? All of them?

"Do you have a drink, Mom?" Riley asked, his mouth full of chips. I passed him my bottle of water from the cup holder. "Thanks."

"So you haven't told your father?"

"You guys have been busy. I didn't want to bother you."

"Busy? What do you mean?"

She looked down, glancing at her brothers, who each shrugged one shoulder, their mouths full of chips. "You guys seem stressed lately."

"We aren't stressed," I lied through my teeth. "We're fine. Why would you say that?"

"You're acting the way Bailey's parents did before they got divorced. All quiet and...weird."

My heart plummeted to my stomach, the guilt weighing on me. I'd thought we'd hidden our problems so well, but apparently not.

Simply *not fighting* in front of our children hadn't been enough to convince them things were going smoothly.

"Is that what you all think?"

Hesitantly, all three heads began to nod.

I puffed out another breath. "You guys, we aren't getting a divorce. And we're never too busy for you. Do you hear me? We've had a lot going on with work, but you know the family comes first. If you need something, all you have to do is come talk to us, okay?"

The begrudging nods came again.

"Your father and I love each other very much. And we both love you all more than anything in the world." I waited. "Okay?"

"Okay."

"Yeah."

"And I love air conditioning," Dylan said, reaching to turn it up once again. This time, I let it stay on full blast, too exhausted to argue.

Their responses told me they didn't believe me, and I was struck by how bad of a job I'd been doing holding us all together. It was all I wanted to do—to make sure they knew how perfect and lucky we were to have each other —but I'd apparently failed in every way.

That had to change.

This was exactly why we needed a weekend away together at the lake house. I'd spent so long feeling like my kids were pulling away from me, but now I realized maybe they'd been feeling the same way.

Did they think *I* was pulling away from *them*?

Was I?

Perhaps the guilt over all we'd done had driven me from them, but now that I knew the issue, I could fix it.

I was a fixer, after all.

CHAPTER TWELVE

PETER

There was a body in our garage.

A decaying body.

It wasn't the first time and I was sure it wouldn't be the last, but this time I had no control over it.

It wasn't my doing.

I didn't know what unfortunate misstep the person—I was assuming it was a woman, but I couldn't be sure—had taken to end up wrapped in a tarp in my garage.

I couldn't press Jim. Couldn't ask too many questions.

After that first night, that had always been the rule between us.

But with the evidence on my property, I had everything to lose here and nothing to gain.

Nothing except his silence, and even that was uncertain.

I knew Jim. I knew that whatever I was doing to make him happy now would only keep him happy until the next favor he needed. I didn't know why I'd fooled myself into believing it would be any different now that we were grown and out of college.

We weren't kids anymore.

We had families, careers...

But neither of us had stopped doing the things that had bonded us back then, and he knew it. He'd used it to control me before and he could still control me with it to this day.

"Did you hear her, Peter?" Ainsley was saying, her voice shrill. When I looked up, I noticed every eye at the table was on me.

"Hm? Sorry, I zoned out. What'd you say?"

Maisy was picking at the food on her plate. "I quit dance."

It took a moment for it to sink in. "Oh... Okay, then." I glanced toward Ainsley, trying to gauge how I was supposed to be reacting. "When did you decide this?"

"Last year," Maisy said. "I haven't started back."

Now I understood the pinched expression my wife was wearing.

"Oh. I didn't realize."

"Me either," Ainsley said. "I found out today when I realized she didn't go to her recital last night. I assumed you were paying for the classes."

"I... Yeah, I assumed you were." I turned to face my daughter. "You should've told us, Maise. Did something happen?"

"Not really." She twisted her hand over her arm. "I just didn't want to do it anymore. Jennessa and Bailey quit, too."

Ainsley was still looking at me, watching my reaction,

but I had no idea if I was acting appropriately. In truth, I never cared if Maisy took the dance lessons in the first place. That was Ainsley's choice. And frankly, her quitting was saving us a ton of money.

"We invested a lot in your dance lessons," Ainsley said, running the tines of her fork across her plate gently. "I just want to be sure you're positive about this decision. Is it the schedule? Or do you want to take a different style this year? What about jazz? Or tap?"

"I just don't want to do it," she said firmly, staring down. "Can we please just drop it?"

"Yes," I said.

At the same time, Ainsley said, "Are you crying?"

I looked across the table at Maisy, spying the glimmer of a tear at the corner of her eye.

"Maisy, what's wrong?" Ainsley pressed up out of her chair in an instant.

"Awkward," Dylan said with a sigh, pushing back from the table.

"Knock it off," I snapped.

"Talk to me," Ainsley whispered as Riley watched intently, his expression filled with genuine concern.

Maisy shook her head. "It's nothing, I swear. I just don't want to do it anymore. Please don't make me."

Ainsley took a hesitant step back, but it was my turn to speak up. "We'd never make you do anything you don't want to, Maise. You know that." She looked at me gratefully, brushing away a tear.

Ainsley watched me and it was obvious she wanted to say more, but instead, she leaned down and kissed the top of Maisy's head. "You know you can

84

always come to us with anything, right? No matter how busy or stressed we seem, you're what matters to us."

"Your mother's right," I chimed in, just as my phone began to buzz in my pocket. I pulled it out, though I desperately didn't want to, and glanced at the screen.

My heart sank.

Not again.

Not right now.

"Can I go to my room?" Dylan asked. His plate had been empty for several minutes and he was already standing, not waiting for an answer.

"Of course," Ainsley said, though I could feel her eyes on me. I considered ignoring the call, but I knew that would only make Jim angry. Sweat beaded at my hairline as I thought back to the body in the garage.

The very, very dead body.

"Peter?" Ainsley called, staring at me strangely.

"I have to take this." I darted out of the room and pressed the phone to my ear. "Yeah?"

"I need another favor."

I huffed, stepping out onto the porch and walking farther into the yard. "Of course you do."

"You home?" He didn't miss a beat.

"You can't come here now. The kids are home and we're in the middle of something. Come by tonight."

"Won't take long."

"It doesn't matter. Look, Jim, you can't keep doing this to me. We agreed on one favor and now we're up to three. When does it end? I've done all that I can do for you. I don't owe you anything else."

"Doesn't seem like you really have a choice, does it?" he said simply.

"What the—" Before I could argue any further, the line clicked and he was gone. "Dammit!" I threw the phone to the ground, anger radiating through me. I shook my head, trying to clear it. How was I going to get out of this—

"Peter?"

I spun around, shocked to see Ainsley there. I guess I shouldn't have been shocked, not knowing her as well as I did.

My wife was always there.

Always around.

I scrambled to pick up my phone, running my hands through my hair. "Sorry..." I didn't know what to say, how to explain what a mess I'd gotten myself in.

"Is everything okay?"

No. Nothing's okay.

"Yep, great."

She pursed her lips, stepping toward me. "It doesn't look great."

Before I could answer, headlights flashed across her face in the dim evening light. I spun around, staring out at the driveway where I could now see the gray truck heading in our direction.

"Who's that?"

I tried to keep my voice calm, to prevent her from hearing the panic I was feeling. "A friend from work."

"The same friend who was here the other night?"

Shit. I'd forgotten about that.

"What's going on, Peter?" she asked, reading the

expression on my face just as Jim's truck came to park in front of us.

I shook my head, forcing a laugh. "Nothing, I told you. It's just work stuff. I'll be back inside in just a minute."

Jim was already out of the truck and walking toward us. When he saw Ainsley, his brows raised, a longing gaze trailing down the length of her body and back up. Fire burned in my belly as I stepped forward, placing myself between them.

"I don't believe I've had the pleasure," he said, outstretching his hand toward her, ignoring me. "James Slater."

Ainsley's eyes fell to me for a second, but I'd sooner tell her to run than give her permission to shake his hand —not after I'd seen the look in his eyes.

"I'll be inside in a minute," I said again, firmly.

To my relief, without shaking his hand, she stepped back, offering a gentle wave. "Nice to meet you." It seemed as though she sensed the danger, or my panic, and I was grateful to see her walking away from us quickly.

Once she was gone, Jim whistled, his brows still raised in a way that had me feeling ill.

"Damn, Greenburg. No wonder you didn't invite me to your wedding."

Yeah, right, that was why.

"What do you need, Jim? I told you we're in the middle of something. This isn't a good time."

It took too long for his eyes and attention to come back to me, and finally, he groaned. "Right. Yeah, well, it's just a small package this time. And this one won't be here long at all. I have a buyer picking it up this weekend."

"This weekend? No, that won't work."

"Why? You got a nail appointment?" He smirked.

"We're…" I thought better of telling him we'd be out of town at the lake house and instead settled on, "We're having company over. It's going to be a whole thing. I can't have anyone else here."

He clicked his tongue thoughtfully, peering around. "Alright, I could probably come pick it up early Saturday morning. What time will everyone start arriving?"

"Friday evening. Saturday's no good for me."

"Well, we're going to have to figure out something, aren't we?" he pressed.

"Where have you been keeping this stuff before now?"

"Here and there," he said with a shrug. "So you can see why this arrangement's a lot better for me."

"Well, it's not an arrangement. You said you needed to keep one thing in the room for a while. I've kept up my end of the bargain and then some. You'll have to find somewhere else to keep this one. I'm sorry." My hands were up in the air as I figuratively washed them of the problem. "You can't keep it here." If he argued, I might have to kill him. Either that, or he'd kill me. But I desperately didn't want either of those scenarios to happen. Not while my kids were home. I'd have to lure him into the room and do it there. I'd have to hope they didn't wonder about my absence too strongly.

He drew in a long breath and the seconds seemed to drag on as I waited to hear his response.

Finally, he said, "Alright, fine. I'll figure something else out."

As he started to walk away, obviously disappointed, I

stepped forward, stopping him. "What about the rest of it? How much longer do you plan to keep it there?"

"I've told you I don't know exactly. I'm figuring things out." He patted my shoulder. "Just enjoy your garden party. I'll take care of the rest." I saw him clock something over my shoulder, his whole demeanor filling with warmth again. When I followed his line of vision, I saw Ainsley's silhouette in the porch light. She'd been watching us. From where she was, I wondered if she could hear us. Surely not.

He tipped his ball cap toward me, then waved at her. "Tell the missus good night from me, would you?"

I didn't respond, but he didn't seem to notice, giving my shoulder a squeeze and making his way back to the truck.

The headlights washed over me as he backed up and turned around, disappearing down the long, curving drive.

The tension disappeared slowly when I'd caught the last glimpse of his taillights. When I turned around, Ainsley had gone back inside.

Still, I knew it was far from over.

These two—my wife and my friend—had enough dirt on me to send me away for the rest of my life. They were dangerous, each in their own way.

Now I just needed to decide whom I was more afraid of.

CHAPTER THIRTEEN

AINSLEY

Peter had hardly listened to a word I'd said at dinner about Maisy suddenly quitting dance class. It wasn't like her to drop her commitments so casually, but he didn't seem to notice or care about the sudden change in her personality.

When he walked outside, I realized why. Though I didn't recognize the man he was meeting, I recognized the look in my husband's eyes: panic.

Ice-cold fear.

I watched them interacting, knowing the weapons were hidden in my husband's secret room, and that the children were just inside. I couldn't do anything but watch and wait.

Wonder what was going to happen.

And then, somewhat anticlimactically, the man left.

When Peter trudged toward the house, I stepped inside, waiting for him to enter.

"Who was that man?" I asked, keeping my voice low the second he'd entered the house.

"I told you, a guy from work."

"You didn't really *tell* me anything, though. That's the point. Who is he? I've never seen him before. Why are you being so secretive? Are you up to something?"

He walked past me, moving toward the kitchen where our wineglasses sat from dinner. As he scooped his up, taking a drink and avoiding my eyes, I pressed on. "Peter, what is going on?"

"Nothing's going on. I was thirsty. Please don't make this into something it isn't."

His cheeks were red, both from the wine and the lies, but I didn't argue. Instead, I waited, which seemed to make him even more uncomfortable than if I'd started an argument.

"Alright, fine. Well, that was Jim. Like I said, we work together and he's been going through some stuff at home. I—"

I folded my arms across my chest, cutting him off. "Like what?"

"It's personal," he lied. "But he'd asked me for some advice awhile back, and he came to tell me how it went. He's really struggling."

"He didn't seem like he was struggling with anything. And why couldn't he just text you? Did that really warrant a visit?" He took another drink, buying himself time, so I went on. "And why couldn't I introduce myself to him? You practically raised your leg and marked me as your territory. You were uncomfortable with him... Why?"

At that, there was an unmistakable hint of a grin on his lips, but he fought it down. "I just didn't want him to think I'd been telling you everything. I was trying to sneak out without you noticing. He's told me a lot in confidence, and I want to hold his trust. That's it."

I raised a brow, staring at him. Sometimes, I just didn't understand him. He chose to lie over the most inconsequential things. Why, when I'd made a point to prove how loyal I was to him—no matter what—did he insist on lying to me?

But there was no point in pressuring him. He'd just shut down further.

No, I needed to find out the truth and then confront him.

It was the only way to do things with Peter. Though for the life of me, I couldn't understand why.

For now, there were more pressing issues. "Fine. So, which one of us is going to talk to Maisy?"

"About what?"

I scoffed, a hand on my hip. Had he truly already forgotten? "About her quitting dance, Peter. What do you mean, *about what*?"

"I thought we'd already moved past that. She said she didn't want to do it anymore, so what's the problem?"

I wanted to throttle him.

"The problem is that she's eleven years old and suddenly she doesn't want to do the thing she's loved doing since she was four. And this change is completely out of nowhere, without even a mention to us about what caused her to come to such a rash decision. It's not normal. It's not like her."

"Who says it's a rash decision? Maybe she thought it through."

"Without talking to us? Not a single time? That doesn't

92

seem likely."

"Her friends aren't dancing, so she doesn't want to. It's not the end of the world. Why are you so upset about it?" He stared at the last of the wine in the bottle, holding it out to me. I shook my head, holding up a hand to say I'd pass, so he poured the remainder into his glass.

"Because this isn't about dance, Peter," I said. "Don't you see that?" No, he didn't see it. I could read that in his expression. He thought I was being irrational. Maybe I was.

What I knew was that our daughter didn't make huge decisions without talking to us. If she'd quit dance, I had to believe there was a reason that went deeper than what she was admitting to us.

Was it peer pressure from her friends?

Had she begun to feel uncomfortable with her body?

Was she struggling with the more advanced routines?

I just didn't know.

"Then what is it about?" he asked, puckering his lips from his last sip of wine.

I folded my arms across my chest, trembling from my own agitation. "She said she didn't tell us because she doesn't feel like she can talk to us anymore."

"She said that?" He appeared skeptical.

"In not so many words," I insisted. "The boys agreed with her, too. They said we seem stressed and busy all the time lately."

"Yeah, well, understatement of the year." He tipped the glass toward me.

"Our kids still need us," I snipped. "No matter what we have going on, we have to keep them a priority—"

"We do—"

"That's not how they see it. A year or two ago, Maisy would've told us about this decision. Now she didn't feel like she could. I'm not saying that's entirely our fault, but now that we know about it, we have to do what we can to fix it."

He contemplated what I'd said, twisting his mouth in thought. "Alright, fine," he said eventually, "but what are you suggesting?"

I was sick from the struggle within me—trying to make sure he understood the severity of the situation while trying not to overreact. "I'm not going to push her tonight, but this is even more reason why we need this trip to the cabin this weekend. We need to remind the kids we're there for them, no matter what. Agreed?"

"Yeah, agreed." His response was halfhearted, but I'd take it.

"We have to keep communication open between us. All of us. Secrets, lies, unspoken truths...they'll all come back to bite us if we aren't careful. If we can't trust this family, if they can't trust us, then what are we even doing?" I drilled home the last part, hoping he'd realize it was meant for him as much as it was for them.

He chuckled, though, not taking it nearly as seriously as I'd meant it. "They can trust us, babe. They know they can. And you can trust me."

So, maybe he had understood.

My lips pressed together in what should've been a smile but felt more like a grimace. Still, he took it and turned to walk away, ruby red splotches on his neck.

Another lie.

CHAPTER FOURTEEN

PETER

I'd never understood people who claimed fresh air brought them peace. For me, there was nothing more stressful than the moment I traded cell phone service for biting insects and blistering heat.

I much preferred the beach trips we'd once taken over the secluded lake house Ainsley had forced us to fork over our life savings to buy years ago. Even then, I'd known we'd never get much use out of it and, truth be told, we'd probably gotten even less than I'd imagined.

But still, if leaving town meant Ainsley was happy for a few hours, I'd suffer through.

We arrived at the lake house just past noon, when the temperature was sweltering and we had to wear the humidity like a coat. The old house's air conditioning unit hummed loudly when Ainsley turned it on, dust flying from its vents.

"It'll just take a bit to cool off," she said, pulling her shirt away from her chest rapidly to fan herself.

The kids spread out, complaining as much as I wanted

to about the heat and the bugs and the smell. Instead, I moved to stand next to her, slipping a hand around her damp waist.

"Come on, guys, it'll be fun. We can go down for a swim while the place cools off. What do you say?"

Maisy was the first to respond. "Okay."

"Anything to get out of here," Riley agreed, panting.

"I'm going to change into my suit." Dylan dropped his luggage on the dusty couch and began riffling through the bag in search of his swimming trunks.

"What do *you* say?" I asked, leaning into Ainsley's hair so close I could breathe in her jasmine scent.

"Sounds good to me," she agreed. She slipped out of my grasp and approached Maisy to ask her, "Can you help me pick out which suit to wear?"

Maisy's eyes lit up at the opportunity, and they disappeared down the hall together, bags in tow.

I was sure Ainsley hadn't meant for it to feel like a snub, but it had. She'd been strange with me since the night Jim had visited, but I didn't understand why. I'd given her a reasonable explanation as to why he was there.

As I pondered what could be wrong, I lugged my own bag to the bedroom Ainsley and I would share and pulled on my trunks and a T-shirt, examining myself in the mirror.

After everything that happened with Stefan, all the truths coming out about our arrangement and how hard she'd worked to keep me, we'd been at our best.

Something about the ferocity with which she'd fought

for me had awakened a hunger in me. A desire for her like I'd never felt before.

For a while, we were more in love than we'd ever been.

Like two lovestruck teens, we couldn't seem to keep our hands off of each other.

But discovering that she knew the truth about me had changed everything. For a while, we were in a sort of limbo. Trying to decide where we fit. Now, it seemed we were more or less back to our normal selves.

Was this just who we were? Maybe the excitement of what we'd done, the adrenaline of our secrets had caused a slight improvement for a while, but that could only hold out for so long.

I sucked in my gut, fussing with my hair. Maybe she wasn't attracted to me anymore. I knew I was still attracted to her.

When I found out she knew the truth about who I was, I thought she'd want to leave me. But she hadn't. She'd stayed and that had landed us...here.

In this...this purgatory of not knowing what was going to happen, not understanding why neither of us had bolted, but being unable to leave. It was worse, somehow.

The waiting.

The wondering.

Worse than the drab existence before.

No matter how hard she tried to convince me she was here to stay, I couldn't believe it. I was waiting for it to all fall apart again.

That was what I deserved.

Or, at least, not this. I didn't deserve to feel so normal.

I didn't deserve her.

"You ready?"

Dylan pushed open the door slightly and I looked away from the mirror, hopeful he hadn't seen how pathetic I was—checking myself out in the mirror as if I were a teenage girl.

"Yep. Yeah."

I followed him out of the room, where they were all waiting.

At first sight of my wife, my throat went dry.

Ainsley's red bikini practically made her porcelain skin glow. My eyes lingered on the deep valley between her breasts, her nipples poking through the material. The ponytail atop her head had me picturing the times I'd tugged at it from behind her, her moaning my name—

I let out a heavy breath, trying to pull myself together.

Jesus Christ.

How long had it been since we'd—

"Okay, let's go," Maisy whined, breaking my trance. "What are we waiting for?"

I was sweating.

God, I was sweating.

Mostly from the heat of the house—which was surely the cause of my sudden insanity—but at least partially from my unexpected, insatiable urge to keep my wife home with me.

To take her into the bedroom and—

"What if you three go ahead and go down, and let your mom and me catch up with you in just a few minutes?"

A few minutes was all I needed.

"Why?" they all asked at once.

"It's a surprise. For dinner." The answer formed as quickly as I said it, but no one seemed to notice.

"Will you be okay?" Ainsley asked Maisy gently, cupping her shoulder.

Maisy nodded, but didn't say a word.

"Stay close to your brothers. We'll be right behind you."

With that, the kids walked out the front door. I watched their heads move past the window as Ainsley approached me.

"Everything okay? What's the surprise?"

I grabbed her, a fire igniting in my belly at her shocked expression, and pulled her toward me, pressing our lips together feverishly.

She jerked out of my grasp, eyes wide. "What are you doing?"

I was stronger than her.

Strong enough to hold her close to me, even as she attempted to get away. It was fun for me to feel her struggle against my strength—always had been. I wasn't stupid, though. I knew when I could get away with it and when it was dangerous to try.

"Let me show you," I whispered, kissing the side of her cheek, her jawline, and her ear.

"Peter, come on, the kids are waiting…" Her protest turned into a throaty whisper.

"So, let them wait." She stopped struggling as much as my hand slid farther down her back. I felt her giving in to me, her struggles becoming less and less strong.

She let out a low moan as I trailed kisses across her neck, nipping at her skin gently.

"I couldn't see you like this and not have you."

She melted, her body practically limp in my arms as she directed my mouth to hers. She gripped my neck, her nails digging into my skin so hard I knew there'd be marks left behind.

I didn't care.

Couldn't.

I wanted—no, *needed*—her. Then and there.

I led us to the bedroom, refusing to stop kissing her, and pushed open the door. My suitcase was still on the bed, and I shoved it out of the way, making room for us without regard for the mess I'd made.

I pulled the triangles of fabric away from her breasts, heat radiating through me at the sight of her.

Lying there.

Waiting for me.

Wanting me.

I slid my swimming trunks down my legs, tearing the fabric of her bikini bottom to the side without warning. I couldn't wait any longer. Not even to prolong the ecstasy on her face as she prepared herself for what was coming.

I slid inside of her, feeling her tense against me, watching her eyes roll back, then close, her jaw tight.

I gripped hold of her shoulders, forcing her body toward me, forcing myself deeper inside of her.

She met my eyes, her gaze filled with passion and longing.

There you are, my girl.

I've missed you.

CHAPTER FIFTEEN

AINSLEY

"Alright, guys. What movie are we watching tonight?" I asked as I cleared away the last of our plates from pizza and ice cream.

"I think I'm just going to go to bed," Dylan said with a yawn.

"What? No family movie night?" Peter crooned. He'd worn the same dumb, sickly satisfied grin since we'd had sex hours before. Deep inside myself, I was fighting the urge to slap it off his expression.

Something had changed between us, but I couldn't put my finger on what it was. I'd always put up with Peter's lies, knowing I could discover the truth easily enough. As much as he'd like to think otherwise, he was a terrible liar. But this time, this lie—hiding the true reason for his coworker's visits late at night—had flipped a switch inside of me.

It was exhausting.

Constantly chasing the truth, wondering when and why the next lie would come...

Spending time worrying about his lies when I should've been focusing on our children, who had obviously noticed my distraction.

Why had I put up with it for so long? Why wasn't I good enough to see the real him no matter how hard I tried?

"Nah," Dylan said. "I'm tired. Julie's coming down tomorrow morning, so I want to be rested."

My back tensed. "What? Julie's coming here?"

"Yeah?" Every eye in the room was on me, and I realized I'd said that entirely too loudly. "Why?"

I stared at my son. "I thought we'd agreed this weekend would be just for family."

"She's not spending the night. Her parents are going to drop her off for the day and come get her after dinner. Dad said it was fine." He jutted a thumb to a bewildered-looking Peter.

"I did?"

"I asked you when we were loading everything into the car this morning, and you said it was fine."

Peter was slow to nod, and I knew he wasn't actually recalling any such conversation. "Right. Yeah. Sorry, yeah. I did say that."

Liar.

"Why does it matter?" Dylan asked. "She's just coming to hang out with me. It's not like she's going to bother you."

I teetered between punishing him and letting it go. Was it worth the fight? "It's not that. I just wasn't planning on having company. I was hoping to get the three of you to myself this weekend. How long's it been since it was just the family together?"

"Like…every night? Come on, Mom. It's bad enough we had to come out here with no service. You can't honestly expect me not to talk to my girlfriend for three days."

"Oh, come on, now. Don't be dramatic," I said, setting the plates back on the table. "You talked to her this morning before we left and you'll talk to her Sunday when we get home. I think you can handle one day without talking."

"You can't honestly expect me to *un*invite her now. Dad said it was fine! I've already told her she can come." He was on his feet then, his voice high-pitched and panicked.

I sighed, wanting to fend off any argument if I could. "Fine, Dylan. It's fine. Whatever." I waved my hand in the air and picked the plates up again, starting to walk from the room as I realized Peter wasn't planning to back me up in the slightest. "What time is she coming in the morning? Does she have any allergies I should know about? I was planning to cook pancakes for breakfast. Is that okay?"

"Could you make them gluten-free?" he asked, wincing.

I shook my head. "It's fine. We'll do eggs. Any other requests for tomorrow?"

Maisy and Riley shook their heads gently as Dylan trudged from the room.

"What about you two? Are you going to stay up and watch a movie with me and your mom?" Peter asked.

"I was planning to go to bed early and read," Maisy said. "I need to finish my summer reading list before school starts back."

"I think I'm just going to go to bed," I said before Riley could answer, though judging by the look on his face, he was planning to decline the invitation, too.

"Don't do that," Peter protested.

"It's fine. I need some rest anyway. The sun zapped me." I gestured toward my sunburned arms.

Riley yawned from where he lay on the couch. "Are you sure?" Peter asked, appearing conflicted. I nodded. "What do you say, bud? Want to watch a movie with your old man?"

"I'm tired too," he said. "Dylan said he'd take me fishing early in the morning before Julie gets here."

"Oh. Well, okay then." Peter stood up begrudgingly, kissing each of their heads.

"You don't have to come with me," I told him. "You can watch a movie if you want."

"No, you're right. We should turn in." He flicked the TV off as the kids began to stand, making their way toward the bedrooms. "Good night, you two. We'll see you in the morning."

"Night."

"Good night."

Peter waited for me to finish up, but once I'd put the plates into the sink and washed my hands, I led the way toward the bedroom. I changed into my pajamas in silence and fluffed the covers, checking to be sure there were no spiders or other critters hiding in the folds of the sheets.

"Listen, I'm sorry I didn't warn you about Julie. Dylan did mention it to me, but I was distracted. I forgot all about it."

"You've been distracted a lot lately," I said simply, slipping under the covers and turning my back toward him as he changed for bed.

"I know. I've had a lot going on."

"Well, that's news to me."

He didn't notice the sharpness in my tone. "It's no big deal, really. Just work stuff, you know?"

"Mhm."

Cool air hit me as he pulled the covers back and lay down next to me. "Everything okay?"

God, sometimes he is so oblivious.

I rolled over to face him, staring at him for a painful few seconds before I spoke. "Peter, why are you with me?"

His expression said I'd caught him off guard. He glanced around, as if he expected he was being pranked, then leaned forward, brushing a piece of hair from my eyes and tucking it behind my ear. "Why am I with you?" he repeated. "What do you mean?"

"Why are we together? Why did you want to marry me? Why do you want to stay with me?"

He gave a dry, confused laugh. "Um, because I love you. Where is this coming from?"

"But do you? Do you love me?"

"Of course I—"

"Because it seems like we just keep coming back to this place of secrets. Over and over again. And I've done all I can to prove to you that you can trust me, to prove that I'm here for you and going to stay here through whatever. I think I've been more than understanding about it all—"

"Is this about Julie?"

"God! No, it's not about Julie. Can you just listen to me?"

"I'm trying, Ains. You're not making any sense."

"Because you haven't let me finish," I said through gritted teeth. "For goodness' sake, just shut up. Stop thinking about how you're going to react or lie your way out of this and just...just listen to what I'm saying."

He inhaled sharply, then released it slowly. His nod was serious. "Okay. Alright. I'm sorry. I'm listening."

"You're lying to me about your friend from the other night."

He blanched, but didn't speak. He was waiting to see what I knew.

"I don't know why he was there, but I know he wasn't there to ask you for relationship advice. What could he possibly have been there to talk to you about that made you unable to tell me the truth? With all I know about you, all you've confessed to me, what could be worse than that?"

He visibly deflated and flopped onto his back, staring up at the ceiling. "You're right."

I knew I was, but I didn't need to confirm that.

"Jim wasn't there for relationship advice. The truth is, I couldn't tell you why he was there."

"Why's that?"

His mouth twisted in thought before he groaned. "Because I was embarrassed."

"Embarrassed, why?"

He lowered his voice, still not meeting my eyes. "I just found out some of the people I work with were questioned about me when Stefan went missing before. During the investigation."

My blood ran cold. *"What?"*

"Yeah, actually, Jim was the one who mentioned it." This was one of the rare times I couldn't tell if he was lying. His cheeks were pink, but perhaps it was due to embarrassment after all. "And so I've been trying to warm him up to me, to find out what exactly he told the police. What exactly they asked."

I masked my inner turmoil with a deceptive calmness. As usual, he had no idea the degree of fear that was raging through me. "Why didn't you say anything to me?"

"Because I was panicked and I didn't want to upset you until I'd figured out whether or not we should be worried."

"But it was back then, right? Not recently."

"Yeah," he said quickly. "Yeah, from what he's said. That was why I didn't want you talking to him. I didn't want him to slip up and say something to you before I'd had a chance to tell you myself. Maybe it was wrong, but I was trying to protect you."

"That still doesn't explain why he had to come over in the middle of the night."

He kept his eyes trained on the ceiling, as if he were reading a script. "Well, the first time he came over, it really was because he had to get paperwork for the job. That was when he mentioned that the police had been to see him. I've been trying to catch him alone to ask him about what they said, but there hasn't been a good chance.

So, I asked him to come over and bring me a few of those papers back just so we could talk."

It made sense, I supposed. In a Peter sort of way.

"And what did he tell you?"

"Just that they asked if he'd ever seen me acting in a way that seemed suspicious. He said he told him no, that I'm a great guy. They asked if I'd ever mentioned Stefan and he hadn't heard of him. And I think they asked about our marriage, if I'd let on that we were having problems, but Jim was kind enough not to mention that."

"So you don't think there's anything to worry about, then?"

"No." He breathed out a sigh of relief, kissing my forehead. "I'm sorry I didn't tell you the truth sooner. I was only trying to protect you."

I allowed him to feel good about himself for the moment, then said, "I don't want you to protect me, Peter. I just want you to be honest with me. I'm trying to do better about being controlling—really, I am. But you have to be up front with me when I ask you about things. We're a team. That's what we agreed."

"Understood." He ran a hand across my cheek again. "Promise."

My eyes danced between his as I tried to decide if I could trust him. I wanted to so badly, and I knew that was my downfall. I'd always wanted to trust him, even when he'd proven to me why I shouldn't.

"Why do *you* want to be with *me*, anyway?" he asked, and I found my eyes blurring, then refocusing as I thought about the question. "You asked me, but you've never told me your answer. Why do you stay with me after everything?"

"Because I love you. And I love our family. And our kids. I don't want to disrupt that. I won't lie to you and say it hasn't been difficult. But I've had time to process and I believe we can get better. If you want to. I believe everything can be fixed."

"But what if I can't?" The vulnerability of the question didn't carry over into his tone. It felt more like a challenge than anything.

"You can. You are."

But was he? The unspoken question was obvious to us both.

"Have you ever thought about leaving me for someone easier?" he asked, reaching out and twisting a strand of hair around his finger.

We were silent for a moment, both staring at each other in complete silence. Finally, I took a breath and said, "When I met you, I thought you were perfect. You charmed my parents, charmed me. You made me laugh. Made me feel safe. You were ready to settle down when I was. You gave me Dylan. You were—are—the best father to him. I have so many good memories of who we used to be. Do you remember how we used to go to restaurants and order our favorite food for each other? Or when we spent the summer exploring every waterfall in Tennessee?"

"Sure." He smiled wistfully.

"So, when I found out what you were doing when you were supposed to be working late all those nights, when I found out what you were capable of—it shook the foundation of the world I knew. I couldn't rationalize how the man I knew, the man I loved, was capable of such terrible things. But it didn't mean I stopped loving you. I stopped understanding you. Maybe I stopped respecting you. But I still loved you, Peter. That never faltered."

Thinking back to those days—watching him playing with our children, helping me clean up after meals, and doing the yard work side by side—all while knowing what he'd done, it was as if I was existing in two alternate realities at once.

For me, so much stayed the same, while at the same time, everything had changed.

It reminded me so much of the early days after bringing Dylan home—our first baby. The moment when our entire world flipped. Everything was simultaneously the same, and yet, completely different. We were the same people, but we'd never feel the same again.

Finding out the truth about the man I'd married put me in an identical foggy state for months, if not years.

Sometimes, I wasn't sure I'd ever left.

"When I was in high school, there was a boy I thought I loved." I rolled my eyes, remembering the feeling well. "My parents hated him."

Peter snorted with a small laugh. "Good."

I narrowed my eyes at him playfully. "Which only made me love him more. You know how my parents are— they make my parenting look lazy."

"That's not true—"

"Oh, but it is. My mom picked out my clothes until I graduated high school. She determined what I did and when, who I hung around with, what sports I played, what I ate, what I wore, what color my nails were painted..."

I'd told Peter most of this, but I hadn't completely laid out a picture of how controlled my childhood was before. "For the longest time, it was just easier to go along with whatever she wanted. But when Ryan came along, it was different. It was the first time I'd ever rebelled. They tried everything to keep me from seeing him: grounding me, taking away my phone privileges, calling the school to ask that we be kept separate. They took away my car and started driving me to and from school again. It was a whole thing, but that only made me more determined to see him. I snuck out constantly, I skipped school... I stopped caring about everything but him."

"You've never told me any of this before."

He was still playing with my hair, and I gently took it from him, needing him to focus on what I was saying. "No. I didn't think it mattered before. It was so long ago." I tucked both my hands up under my cheek on the pillow. "But after we'd been dating for a while, Ryan started getting into trouble with drugs and drinking."

"How old was he?"

"Nineteen at that point. I was seventeen. Watching him going down that road was...terrifying, to put it mildly. I don't think I've ever felt so out of control. I did everything I could to bring him back, but I couldn't. He wouldn't listen to me... There was no reasoning with him. He thought he could take care of himself, but anyone could see from a distance it was going to end badly. And it did. He overdosed just before his twentieth birthday."

"I'm so sorry," Peter said, drawing in a breath. "I had no idea."

"That was when I realized why my mom tried to control me as much as she did. Because to her, control was love. She was keeping me safe. As much as I hated it then, I wished I'd been more like her when it counted. I thought if I'd been better at controlling him, I might've saved him."

His eyes softened, giving me a pitying look that made me feel sick. "You know that's not true."

"I know I couldn't have saved him, yes, but then I met you, and I later discovered your secret and it was like my chance with Ryan all over again. I don't think I ever put it together until recently. I just kept thinking about him— not because I miss him or wish I was still with him, but because this situation makes me feel like I'm reliving all of that. It's like my second chance."

I stared at him, wondering if I was making any sense. "All I want to do is save you, Peter. From yourself. That's why I am the way that I am. That's why I'm with you. Because to walk away, to leave you with your demons until you destroy yourself..." I trailed off, shivering. "I'm not sure I'd survive it."

He wrapped his arms around me, pulling me in close. "You'll never have to, Ains."

I rested my cheek against his chest, inhaling his scent. This was where I was the happiest. The safest. Despite all our issues, Peter was the only place I'd ever felt at home.

"Which is why I want to create a new arrangement." My voice was muffled against his chest, and I felt him stiffen, then pull back.

"What? I thought we'd agreed that was a horrible idea."

"Not like before. Well, sort of like before. An...amendment to the arrangement."

His hand slid down my arm, his expression skeptical. "I'm listening."

"I want to do it with you."

"Do what?" One brow drew down.

"*It*," I stressed, trying to force myself to say the words that had been swirling in my mind for the past few days. "Instead of sleeping with other people, I want to help you kill other people."

CHAPTER SIXTEEN

PETER

It was madness.

We'd agreed it could never happen again.

We'd agreed I was going to get better.

That I would stop hurting people.

But now she was...what? Giving me permission?

Last time I'd gotten permission to do something previously off-limits, it had been a setup. But this time, what could she be setting me up for? She already knew the truth about everything. Already had all the evidence she could need to get me into trouble. She already had me at her beck and call.

But this couldn't be real.

And, even if it was, there was no way in hell I was going to go through with it.

Knowing that Ainsley knew my secret was painful enough. Having her watch me kill Stefan, even if it was exactly what she wanted, was mortifying.

Killing was private.

Intimate.

Ending a life wasn't meant to be a spectator sport.

When it was done for pleasure, I meant for the moment to be only between the two of us. Cat and mouse. Killer and victim.

Adding Ainsley into the mix was too dangerous.

Still, I couldn't stop myself from thinking of it.

There was something erotic about picturing her taking part.

Something wrong, too.

I couldn't decide how I wanted to proceed.

We'd cut the conversation short the night before when I'd asked for time to consider it. She was offended, but I couldn't say any more then. My head wasn't clear when I was with her.

It had never been clear—*would* never be clear—in her presence.

"I'm just going to see if the kids want a snack," she said, interrupting my thoughts as she bustled past the recliner I was sitting in, a basket of food in her hands.

"I'll come with you." I jumped up, following close behind her. Like Dylan had said, Julie arrived in time for breakfast that morning, but she'd only eaten a few small bites before the two of them changed into their swimming suits and headed down to the lake, towels slung over their necks.

The girl was so quiet I'd probably heard her speak three sentences total, and only when she was spoken to. Dylan, on the other hand, had spoken more than I'd heard him in years. Perhaps trying to keep us from talking directly to Julie too much.

Still, I knew it had just about destroyed my wife not to

get to spend most of the morning talking to the new girl in our son's life.

I was supposed to be the dad in the scenario, to pat him on the shoulder encouragingly and tell Ainsley it would all be alright, but in truth, I was curious about her, too.

It was Dylan's first real girlfriend, and that meant something special to us all.

"Do you really think they're hungry?" I asked, trying to keep up with Ainsley's quick pace. It was only about two hours since we'd had breakfast, so I had to imagine whatever we were doing had little to do with hunger.

"They might be. I just want to check in and be sure they're doing okay."

"You know they're going to be fine, right? I mean, Maisy and Riley are there, too. It's not like they're alone."

When I looked at her, her expression was pinched, as if she were concentrating hard on something important. It struck me then—was she worried about what Dylan and Julie might be doing, or was she worried about what Dylan might be doing *to* Julie? Did she worry about him turning out like I had? Turning into me?

The thought was sobering.

But she didn't know the truth about how it had all started.

If I'd never met Jim, if he hadn't shown me the power that came with it all, I might never have turned into the monster I was.

It wasn't genetic...

My son would never be what I was. I had to believe that.

I wanted to assure her of this, but I couldn't manage to form the words. They were painful. Everyone hopes their children will turn into some better version of themselves. It's why we search for ourselves in their tiny features when they're newborns.

But to hope, like I had to, that they'd end up nothing like me, was unexpectedly painful. I guess I'd never thought about it until that moment.

We were nearing the edge of the water, both of us searching the shoreline for the kids. At first I didn't see them, but eventually, I heard a nearly unfamiliar giggle.

Ainsley heard it at the same time and we turned abruptly, headed in the direction of the sound. They were gathered together, the four of them—Julie sitting close to Dylan on the ground at the base of a tree while Maisy and Riley sat down from them a bit, each of them staring out at the choppy water.

"Where did you hear that?" Dylan was asking, his face turned slightly toward Julie, tone skeptical.

We were closer now, though they still hadn't noticed us.

"A lot of girls have been talking about it. I'm surprised you hadn't heard, Maisy. I heard he sent one of the pictures to Nikki Schneider."

"Pictures of what?" Dylan asked.

Julie snorted, dragging a twig through the dirt at her feet. "Well...not his face."

Ainsley stopped short, placing a hand out to stop me as well. It felt wrong, overhearing a conversation I was sure wasn't meant for us, but I couldn't help being intrigued. Who were they talking about?

"Sick," Riley said.

"I'll bet it's all shriveled and nasty," Dylan chimed in.

"He's not *that* old," Julie argued.

"He's our parents' age," Dylan argued.

Ainsley and I exchanged a glance, not daring to move.

Who were they talking about?

"Well, if they have pictures, they should turn him in," Maisy said, keeping her arms wrapped around her legs.

"I doubt it. Nikki was bragging about it. I got the impression she sent him a few pictures herself. You really haven't heard anything? I've heard Bailey Jones was one of the girls he's been sleeping with. Aren't you friends with her?"

Beside me, Ainsley sucked in a sharp breath. Bailey was eleven years old, the same age as Maisy. Not old enough to be sleeping with anyone. And certainly not someone my age.

A protective rage filled my stomach.

Someone needed to report this. I wanted to go forward, to demand they tell me what they were talking about, but I feared if I did, I might never know the truth. Ainsley seemed to be struggling with a similar train of thought.

"Shut up! You have no idea what you're talking about. You shouldn't say stuff like that when you obviously don't know anything," Maisy said, the anger in her voice palpable. She stood abruptly, dusting her hands across the seat of her shorts.

"Don't snap at her," Dylan shouted back defensively.

"I'm sorry. I was just saying what I'd heard—"

"Well, what you've heard is shit—"

I'd never heard my daughter curse before, and that alone was a kick to the gut. Before I'd had a chance to recover, Maisy had turned around and stopped short, staring at us in horror.

"Mom? Dad?"

Ainsley met my eyes briefly as we both contemplated what we should say or how we should move forward. It was as if the ground had crumbled beneath us. I could see it on each and every one of our faces. In the end, it was my wife who navigated us through. She dropped her arms in front of her, the basket dangling near her knees.

When she spoke, her voice was soft but shaken.

"Let's go inside for a bit, Maisy. We... I think we should talk."

CHAPTER SEVENTEEN

AINSLEY

"You're not in trouble, sweetheart. You just need to tell us the truth."

"But I *have* told you the truth," Maisy screamed, her cheeks red with frustration and glistening with fresh tears.

"So, you have no idea what Julie's talking about? Bailey hasn't mentioned anything about it at all?"

"No," she whined, swiping her hands across her eyes. "Please just stop! She doesn't know anything!"

"Okay." I put my hands up, trying to calm her down. "Let's just breathe." I gestured toward the bed and we sat down. Peter was likely lingering just outside the door, but I knew if I had any shot of getting her to open up, talking to her alone was it.

She sat down slowly, her breathing erratic as she sobbed. "Okay, let's just start with who Julie was talking about in the first place. Who was the man?"

Her face wrinkled. "It's all just a stupid rumor, Mom. Please don't make me talk about it. It's disgusting!"

"I'm sorry, but I can't just let it go. If it is a rumor, we'll figure out how to get it stopped. I'm not going to be mad at you, I just want to help Bailey."

She sniffled, looking up at me. "What will happen to them?"

"Happen to who, baby?"

"To the girls…"

Something in the quiver of her voice had my insides squirming. "So, it *is* true, then?"

She placed her face in her palms. "I don't know."

"Well, what *do* you know?"

She was quiet.

"Do you know who Julie was talking about?"

Face still in her palms, she nodded.

"You can trust me. I only want to help."

"I don't want anyone to get into trouble." She broke down into sobs then and I pulled her to my chest, smoothing her hair down against her temples as I had when she was a small child. She was too young to be dealing with this. It broke my heart to even broach the subject.

"I promise you, you won't get into trouble. Bailey either. None of your friends… You've not done anything wrong. But you have to talk to me so I can fix this."

She shook her head against my chest. "I really didn't want to quit dance, Momma."

The words chilled me to my core. "Wha—"

"It was Coach Chris."

No.

My throat went dry, the hair on my arms standing on end. "What are you talking about?"

The dance coach I'd trusted to teach our daughter over half of her life. The man who'd taken the girls to dance competitions. The man who'd brought her home when we had to work late or kept our daughter back for an extra session when she wasn't nailing her routine.

"What did he do, Maisy?" I said, praying Peter was standing outside the door and hearing every word I was. If not, I might be convinced I'd misunderstood. "He was the one sending those pictures?"

She pulled away, meeting my gaze with such wide-eyed innocence it broke my heart.

"Yes. To some of the girls on the team."

"Did he send any to you?"

She shook her head, and relief broke through the concrete boulder in my chest.

"Did he...did he touch you? Did he hurt you?"

"No," she confirmed.

"But... He *did* do something to Bailey?"

Her head hung with a regretful nod.

"What did he do to Bailey?"

I hated myself for feeling relief that it was someone else's child. "I don't know when it started. He was keeping her after practice and doing private sessions for a while. Then it was nearly every day. Every practice. She didn't tell us what was happening, but then in health class we talked about...well, you know."

I didn't know. I wasn't sure if I wanted to know. "Talked about what?"

"Diseases and stuff." She wouldn't meet my eyes. I was almost thankful for it.

"We didn't know about all of that... I mean, I knew

you could get pregnant or whatever, but... I guess it scared Bailey, and she told us."

"She told you they'd been having sex?"

"And other stuff."

I was going to be sick. I placed a hand to my stomach to keep from throwing up.

"And did you tell anyone? Any teachers or parents?"

"He told her no one would understand. She thinks they're in love."

"Maisy, you know it's impossible for a child to love an adult in that way. He's abusing her. What he's doing is illegal and completely wrong." I looked away, tears filling my eyes at how terrified she must be. She was just a child. They were all just children. "Is that why you left dance? Because of what he was doing to her?"

"Sort of." She wrung her hands together in her lap.

"Sort of?"

"Coach asked me to start staying late with him for practices last year. I stayed for one, and he followed me into the locker room. He kept saying something about a tag on my leotard and how he needed to help me get it off."

I was going to pass out. I was sure of it.

"Did he?"

"No," she said quickly. "It was after Bailey had told me what he did to her. I was scared, and I told him you were waiting for me outside. After I told Bailey what happened, she was angry with him. That was when she decided to drop out of dance. I was too scared to tell you anything, so I stuck with it—"

"Oh, honey—"

"But then he started pulling me out of routines and criticizing me in front of everyone. He moved me to the back of every formation. I just thought it was going to keep getting worse."

We were both crying then, and I pulled her into my chest. "You did the right thing. Do you hear me?" I cupped her face, drawing her away from me to meet her eyes. "Thank you for telling me. I'm so sorry you had to deal with that, but I promise you I'm going to handle it."

"Mom, you can't tell anyone." If possible, her face went even paler. "If everyone knew what happened...well, you heard what Julie said about Bailey. The rumors are everywhere. I don't want anyone talking about me. We dropped out of dance, we're safe. Please just let it go. Please."

"Maisy, I can't do that. You're safe, yes. But there are other girls out there who aren't. Kids. Maybe girls who don't have a parent to talk to. We have to report him. Bailey's parents should know what's happening. We need to get the police involved. I have an obligation to report this as a parent... You're all just children."

"No." She looked horrified. "No, you can't! Please! You said I could trust you!"

"You can trust me—"

"You said you wouldn't tell—"

"I never said that. Let's just take a breath—"

She stood, her arms at her sides. "I can't believe you. You lied to me. I should've never told you. You're going to ruin my life."

"Maisy, please—" I reached for her, but she was already storming away.

"I'll never tell you anything else if you do this," she warned. "Bailey will never forgive me. Everyone will hate me. I thought I could trust you!"

"Sweetheart, that's not true. No one will hate you. Please, wait. Let's talk about this—"

But it was no use. She'd swung open the door and stormed out, and I was left reeling with everything I'd learned and had no clear path forward.

I remembered being Maisy's age, remembered when everything felt like the end of the world, but this was so much bigger than anything I'd dealt with at this age.

I gripped my fists in front of me, staring at the empty doorway.

We'd trusted him.

We'd counted on him, and he'd betrayed us.

I wanted to kill him.

To make sure he'd never hurt anyone else.

I wanted to go back in time and kill him before he'd ever had the chance to step foot into my daughter's life.

A sickly feeling washed over me as I watched Peter appear in the doorway. I knew from a single glance that he'd heard everything.

He nodded at me slowly, his eyes bloodshot and wild.

"They're children, Peter. I know you haven't made up your mind about what I proposed, but...this is a special circumstance. You heard her, she'll never forgive us if we tell. We have to handle this." My body trembled with rage, my breathing erratic. My vision tunneled as I struggled to focus on him. "I physically can't breathe until he's taken care of."

His response came in the form of an exhale, as if he'd been waiting for me to say exactly that. "Then we'll take care of him."

CHAPTER EIGHTEEN

PETER

Rather than staying at the lake house for the entire weekend like we'd intended, we headed home Saturday night in decidedly less pleasant spirits than we'd arrived.

Maisy had been quiet for the rest of the day, audibly regretting ever telling Ainsley the truth about her dance coach. Ainsley and I were attempting to convince her things would be alright and stewing separately on what we'd learned as we tried to decide our best course of action.

Whatever we decided, it would be less vicious than what I wanted to do to him. If I'd been able to leave without getting caught, I'd have already torn the man limb from limb.

What kind of a sick freak could do that to kids?

I wasn't missing the irony of the situation, for the record, but my victims were always adults. I'm not claiming to be a saint, but I did, at least, have some sense of morality.

We drove down the driveway in silence, everyone seemingly lost in their own thoughts. As the house came into view, I reached up, tapping the button to open the garage and froze.

The light was on.

It had definitely been off when we left... Hadn't it?

We'd left in the middle of the day. There would've been no reason for it to be on.

I glanced at Ainsley in the passenger seat, but she didn't seem to have noticed, still lost in her own world.

"Did we leave the garage light on?"

"Hm?" she asked, still not really listening.

"The light..."

I parked the car in the garage and stepped out first, looking around defensively. The shelf was still in place, nothing else appeared to be moved, but still, I found chills lining the back of my neck. The kids slid out of the car next. I could smell the lake water, sunscreen, bug spray, and sweat on them, even from where I was.

Dylan made it to the door, but I hurried forward, key outstretched. "Wait!" I tugged at the handle, grateful to see it was still locked. Ainsley yawned behind me, oblivious to my panic. When the doorknob turned, I stepped in front of Dylan, trying to squeeze my way inside first. "Wait," I warned again.

"What's the matter with you? You gotta take a dump or something?" he teased, stepping back and letting me through.

"Shh..." I whispered, turning back to face them. "Wait here."

Now I had Ainsley's attention. She cocked her head to the side, sensing the seriousness in my expression.

"Get back in the car, kids." Her tone carried weight, and none of them bothered to argue.

"What's going on?" Maisy asked just before I heard the car door shut. I was already moving forward, opening the closet next to the garage door and grabbing an old lamp I'd been meaning to throw away. I held it above my head as a weapon, preparing to walk up the stairs with as much bravery as I could muster.

I heard footsteps approaching me from behind and turned around, shocked and relieved to see Ainsley there, following closely. "What is it? Should I wait with the kids?"

I pressed my fingers to my lips, trying to listen.

She stayed still, keeping watch through the open door on the children waiting in the car. I lost sight of her as I made it upstairs and rounded the corner, making my way cautiously down the hall. I checked each of the bedrooms, the laundry room, and the bathroom. I pulled back the shower curtain and the regular curtains, checking in closets and under beds. In the living room, I checked behind the entertainment center and under the table in the dining room.

To my relief, our house appeared empty and untouched. So, perhaps we had just left the light on, after all.

The tension had just begun to leave my body as I returned to the garage, giving Ainsley a wave with a puff of air from my lips. "False alarm. Everything's fine."

"Are you sure? What happened?"

"I don't know; it was probably silly. It's just... I don't remember leaving the garage light on, do you?"

She spun around, peering into the garage. "I don't remember it, no. Why? Do you think someone's been here?"

I gave an embarrassed laugh. "No, I guess not. Like I said, it was silly. I just had a bad feeling and overreacted."

She watched me for an extra second. "Are you sure?"

"Yeah, the coast is clear."

I watched as she backed away from me slowly, moving back toward the kids, and motioned for them to get out of the car.

"What was that about?" Riley asked, obviously shaken.

"It's nothing, sweetie. Your dad was worried someone might have tried to break in because the light was on. But he's checked it out now and we're safe."

"You thought someone was inside our house?" Maisy gasped, her voice filled with horror.

"Bit of an overreaction. Everything's fine."

"Are you sure?" Even Dylan seemed hesitant to go in.

"Promise, bud." I patted his head. "Help your mom and me with the bags."

With that, we loaded up the luggage and carried it inside. Once everyone had set off on their own, I ventured back to the garage. It was probably nothing, but I had to check, just to be sure.

I shut the door behind me and crossed the garage toward the wall. With a quick check over my shoulder to make sure I wasn't being watched, I nudged the shelf out of the way and began to press the bricks in, waiting for the wall to open.

Once it had, I stepped inside, my breathing catching in my throat. The body had begun to decay, its rancid smell filling the room. I needed to move it to the freezer, though I'd been warned not to touch it. But now, I wasn't sure that would even be possible.

In fact, it seemed impossible I would ever locate the freezer again. The room was filled with boxes I'd never seen before. As if a moving truck had hauled in a whole home's worth of packages and dropped them in every nook and cranny it could find. I could hardly step inside, only a very narrow path through the center of the room still available.

"What the hell?" I muttered under my breath.

I stepped forward, no longer caring about our agreement, since he obviously didn't care, either. I tore open the first box, spying the stacks of passports, ID cards, and social security cards.

Fakes, I assumed.

All of them.

I pieced through them, shaking my head before dropping the box and tearing open the next one. It contained more of the same.

What the hell?

I had no idea what sort of things Jim was into, but I knew they likely weren't good. Still, this came as a shock.

I suspected he'd crossed further lines since we were in college—that he was dealing harder drugs, involving himself with more dangerous men, and probably hurting a lot more people. But keeping him close to me had always kept me protected.

We weren't friends anymore, but I sent him a good amount of work. We'd been cordial. Pleasant.

He stayed in his world and I stayed in mine.

As long as that remained the unspoken agreement, I was fine with it. But this...this was crossing a line I didn't even know I had.

The next box was filled with three briefcases, all locked. I could hazard a guess that they contained weapons of some sort. The next was filled with vials of a clear liquid. I dropped them back into their boxes, backing out of the room, my stomach roiling.

What had he done?

What was he thinking?

This couldn't happen. Once out of the room, I shut the wall, then I stepped out of the garage and pulled out my phone, dialing his number. I had no idea what I was going to say to him, only that I needed to put an end to this now.

"Yeah?" he answered, his mouth full of food.

"What the hell, Jim?"

"Well, hello to you too, sunshine."

"What have you done? Why is my room full of even more of your boxes? I never gave you permission to—"

He inhaled, swallowing his food loudly. "You lied to me, Greenburg."

"What are you talking about?"

"You lied to me and said you'd have people over this weekend. And you didn't."

"Why did you come here? You were trespassing! You had no right to come onto my property. This has gone far enough."

He chuckled, sending my blood pressure through the roof. My vision was beginning to tunnel, my head throbbing.

"Do you think this is funny?"

"No. I don't, actually. I don't think it's funny that you lied when you know how much is on the line."

"What exactly are you going to do? You're going to turn me in? Really? After everything we've been through? After you've done so much worse shit and for so much longer. What a fuckin' hypocrite," I spat, pacing the ground.

"Who says I'm going to rat you out? I ain't no snitch, Greenburg. You oughta know that."

"So what do you want, then? I can't have this stuff here, man. I need that space. My wife and kids are here." I glanced over my shoulder at the thought of them, pleased to see I was still alone. "You can't bring anything else here, and you can't leave all of this. It has to go. Whatever else it is you want—money, better projects at work, whatever— we'll work it out."

"Whatever I want, hm?" he asked, sucking his teeth.

"Name it."

"It's funny you say that because I actually have been thinking about something else I want." A knot formed in my stomach as I waited for the bomb to drop.

"Ever since I saw that wife of yours—" He groaned. "*Uh-huh!* I ain't been able to take my mind off of her."

"You'd better think long and hard about what you're going to say."

"Oh, I have," he said, his voice a low growl. "Long and hard." He drew out the words, and I felt my free hand clamp into a fist involuntarily. I imagined it was his throat.

"Forget it."

"You haven't even heard my proposition yet."

"I've heard enough."

"You never know, it could be a good deal."

"She's my wife, you sick fuck. The mother of my kids. If you think for one minute I'm going to—"

"I just want one night with her. One night, and this all goes away."

"No way. Not gonna happen."

"Suit yourself," he said, taking a drink of something and swallowing loudly. "But those are the terms. One night with your wife—no rules—and everything goes away. The room could be cleared out tomorrow."

I nearly dropped the phone; my hands were shaking so hard. The rage was boiling over, my stomach clenching with his every word. "You will never touch her, do you hear me? Not as long as I'm still breathing. If you so much as come near her, I swear to God, I'll—"

"You'll what, Greenburg?" He chuckled to himself. "Where's your sense of fun? It could be like the old days."

"I don't seem to recall things working out too well for the women in our old days."

"Nah, now, this wouldn't be that. I'd bring her back to you alive and well… If not a little sore."

"Fuck you—"

He laughed, cutting me off. "Suit yourself, but take some time to think about it, okay? You have twenty-four hours to decide. If I don't hear from you, I'll have another shipment being delivered next weekend. I'll be around, unloading and loading stuff when I need to. Might have to send a few of my guys in when I get a bigger shipment. This one was a bitch to do myself. You can leave the door open if you want, but...well, you know, we can find our way in if we need to. Perks of building the room, I guess."

"You're crazy if you think—"

"Twenty-four hours."

The call ended, and my chest swelled with outright horror.

Now what was I supposed to do? There was no way I was going to let him have any amount of time with Ainsley, not that she'd agree to it anyway. And I couldn't have him and his *guys*—whatever the hell that meant—showing up to my house whenever they wanted to when my kids were home.

I already had one murder to plan; I desperately didn't need another.

But here I was, with my hands tied.

There was no choice, really.

And now, I had a ticking clock on top of it all.

Twenty-four hours.

CHAPTER NINETEEN

AINSLEY

One problem at a time.

We could only solve one problem at a time.

Peter had taken Dylan to meet Julie, Riley was out for the day with a few of his friends, and Jennessa and her mother had come to pick up Maisy first thing that morning.

I tried not to take it personally that we'd only been home from our family bonding trip for twelve hours—most of those sleeping hours—when each of my children chose to bolt.

I needed to talk to Maisy further. I felt awful letting her leave, but in truth, I was grateful for the quiet to let myself process and decide how we were going to move forward.

Well, that's not entirely true. I knew how we were going to proceed.

Peter and I were going to kill him.

Period.

The sooner he took his last breath, the better.

But would we make him confess first? Would we ask for the names of all of his victims? Would it be random? Would he know why he was going to die?

Most importantly, how were we going to do it without getting caught?

I was having flashbacks of the experience with Stefan —blood and evidence, panic and fear, cops and knocks on doors, long, sleepless nights...

I didn't want to relive that, but this time would be different.

Then, I'd needed to keep Peter in the dark about why Stefan had to die. I needed him to see that we could rely on each other. I wanted him to finally come clean to me about everything—all his secrets—in order to save us.

When he hadn't, I'd finally had to confront him.

This time, everything was on the table. I knew Peter could get rid of the body, just like he had before.

I knew he could clean it up.

I knew we had a place to hide it until that time.

What I didn't know was how both of us would hide our disappearance for any stretch of time, all while constructing some sort of alibi in case the police came around.

I wondered about the first time Peter killed someone.

Had he had these same fears?

I wanted him to trust that I was on board completely. I wanted him to trust me. That meant hiding my fears, my questions, and trusting that he could lead us through it.

Just last night, he'd suggested that maybe I should let him handle everything.

That couldn't happen.

I was too invested. I needed to watch him die. I needed to see his pain after what he'd done to Maisy and her friends.

I shuddered to think it could be so much worse.

No, I had to prove it to Peter—and to myself—that I could handle it. All of it. This felt like my initiation. If I could pass the test, he'd finally let me all the way in.

Luckily, I'd always been a fan of tests and challenges. I could do this.

A knock on the door drew me out of my thoughts, and I glanced at the clock. It was just after eleven.

Peter should've still been dropping Dylan off. I didn't expect him to be back home for the next hour.

I drained the last of the tea from my mug and stood from the table, making my way into the living room. I moved the curtain aside, peeking out the glass, and staring at the familiar face.

"Hello?" I asked as I opened the door. The man Peter had been talking to in the driveway just a few nights earlier stood in front of me. He was tall and blond, with a charming smile despite a single, silver tooth, and piercing eyes that shot straight through you. He was more handsome than Peter in the traditional sense—though I'd never admit that to him—but something felt cool about this stranger. As if something was missing inside of him.

A corner of his mouth upturned, and I spotted the rest of his nearly perfect white teeth. He shoved a hand inside his pocket, looking past me and into the house. "You must be the missus."

I gripped the door. "I'm...Ainsley. You're Peter's friend, aren't you? From work?"

"That's me. Only, we go way back. I'm Jim."

I held out a hand, ignoring the shiver of panic that shot through me. "Nice to meet you. Officially."

"The pleasure's all mine." He sandwiched my hand between both of his, his skin lingering on mine for too long. Something lit up in his eyes, and I pulled back with a wave of apprehension gnawing at my insides. I held on to the door tighter. "Well, Peter's not home right now. He should be back soon."

He chuckled, his eyes lifeless and cold. "It'll be a while, I'd say. He's on his way to my place. About an hour outta town."

Was that true? Peter hadn't mentioned going anywhere but to Julie's house.

"Oh," I squeaked out. "Well, I was right in the middle of something. Maybe you could come back when he's home…" I started to shut the door, but he shoved his boot inside, stopping me abruptly.

"Actually, I'm here to see *you*."

"Me?" I rested a hand on my chest.

"Yes, ma'am." He glanced behind him. "Mind if I come inside?"

My pulse quickened, beating erratically at the deep timbre of his voice. "Um…"

His boot was still forcing the door open with no sign of relenting. If I fought him, he'd force his way inside anyway. I stepped back, trying to appear gracious.

"Okay, sure. Excuse the mess. We're just getting back from a trip."

"Looks like you got a little bit of a tan," he said, his eyes lingering on my shoulder, then trailing down the neckline of my tank top and over my legs.

I covered my shoulder instinctually, looking away as I moved to shut the door, turning my back to him. "Yeah, maybe." I felt him step forward, so close to me I could feel his body heat.

I spun around, inching backward until I could move no farther. I felt like an ant he was waiting to squash. "S-so, what can I do for you?" I asked, sliding out from between him and the door, not daring to turn my back to him again.

"Well, I have a few ideas."

Cold fear pounded in my ears.

"Peter really should be here any time..." I warned, praying it was true.

"We've got time."

"Time for what?" I played innocent, continuing to make my way toward the kitchen.

"Peter and I have an agreement."

"W-what kind of agreement?" My body trembled with fear, and I tried not to let him see it, crossing my arms to hide my fists.

"Come here and let me show you." His eyes trailed down the length of my body again, more aggressively this time.

I took two more steps backward, shaking my head. "I'm sorry, I think maybe you have the wrong idea."

His grin never wavered, though somehow it seemed as if his eyes darkened. "I don't have the wrong idea at all, sweetheart. I've seen the way you look at me."

Near enough to the kitchen, I turned and bolted, running away from him with as much speed as I could muster. Seeing me run made it fun for him, I could hear that in the erratic, excited way he was breathing. He hurried after me, entering the kitchen just seconds after I had.

But it was seconds too late.

He stepped onto the plastic drop cloth I'd laid out, realizing what was happening just as he did so.

He glanced down at the crunch under his feet, then back up just as I pulled the knife from the pocket of my pants. I lunged forward, swinging it with a single, swift motion. It sliced his throat, blood spurting onto the drop cloth I'd carefully coated the room in, the pieces I'd taped to the cabinets and refrigerator.

His hand went to his neck, fingers suddenly stained crimson as he attempted to stanch the bleeding.

"You...*bitch*..." He sputtered, his voice garbled as he fell to the floor.

I stood over him, knife in hand and at the ready, but I knew I wouldn't need to use it again. One slice, to the exact right spot, was all it took. I'd gotten lucky, but it had worked.

He was on the ground now, writhing in pain and fear. I relished the panic on his face, panic like I knew he'd enjoyed seeing on my own. Even if it was all an act.

"That's right," I whispered, lowering myself down closer to him. "This...*bitch*." Then, just for good measure, I lifted the knife one last time and plunged it into his neck, next to the already open wound.

I waited and I watched, remembering what Peter had said about killing people. Finally, I saw the appeal.

It was empowering.

Magical.

For once, *I* was the whole damn world.

CHAPTER TWENTY

PETER

B y the time I got back to my house from Jim's, I was all pent up. I'd spent most of last night and all of this morning preparing to murder one of my longtime friends.

I'd loaded up my tools in the car—a knife, a tarp, the cleaning supplies—and I'd driven the hour and a half to his place.

Upon arrival, I'd realized he wasn't there.

Did he expect me to show up and try something? Maybe.

But some part of me had to believe he'd never expect me to try something so bold.

So, now, I'd built myself up for the murder—so excited I could practically hear his last breaths, feel the blood specks on my skin—only to be completely let down when it didn't happen.

It was the emotional equivalent of blue balls.

As I neared the house, I spied Ainsley waiting on the

porch swing, a mug of tea in her hands. I loved seeing her that way. So calm. So peaceful. Oblivious, even.

If only she knew what I was going through to protect her.

I climbed from the car and made my way up the porch to join her.

"Whatcha thinking about?"

She'd changed clothes from when I'd seen her last, and up close I noticed red flecks in her auburn hair. Had she been painting?

"Where were you?" she asked, her eyes darting to meet mine.

"Sorry it took so long. I stopped by the store to look for that coffee creamer I like, but they were out. I went to half a dozen places and no one had it."

She nodded stiffly, standing and walking past me.

"Headed inside?"

"Yeah." She pushed the door open behind her, letting me grab hold of it to follow her in. "I should warn you, it's kind of a mess in here."

"What do you—" Before I could finish the question, I stepped through the door into the house and every nerve in my body lit up. I smelled the rusty iron scent of blood.

A lot of blood.

"Ainsley?"

She ignored me, moving through the living room as if she didn't smell a thing. Suddenly, I thought back to the specks of red in her hair. "Ainsley?"

No. It wasn't possible.

I didn't have time to process my suspicions. Seconds later, I was in the kitchen and they were confirmed. In the center of the floor, a body lay wrapped in clear, plastic cloth. Surprisingly, the room was otherwise clean.

I stared at my wife, then at the body.

It wasn't possible.

It had to be a joke.

She wasn't capable of this.

"What happened?"

"Your friend came by." Her arms were wrapped around herself, the mug of tea still gripped in one hand.

"Friend?" *Jim.* My stomach knotted. "What happened? Did he…did he hurt you?"

At that, she snorted, her brows raising in amusement. "He tried. I stopped him, no thanks to you."

"I don't understand… He wasn't supposed to be here."

"Did you honestly think he would just be waiting at home for you to come by? Seriously, Peter? Use your head."

"I—" How did she know I'd gone to his house? How did she know anything? "I don't understand."

She snapped her fingers, as if she'd just thought of something. "I'll tell you what I don't understand. I don't understand why you wouldn't just tell me what was going on. Why didn't you tell me what he wanted, Peter? It would've saved us all a lot of trouble."

"How do you know what he wanted?" I demanded, still completely lost.

"Do you honestly think I haven't learned to listen in on your calls by now?"

What the hell? "Listen in? What do you mean? Do you have my phone bugged? Or the house? Or—"

"It doesn't really matter. What matters is that I

shouldn't have to do it. You should be honest with me so it's not necessary. But you've proven time and time again that it *is* necessary. If you'd told me what was going on, we could've set him up. Had him come here and killed him together. Like a team. Like the team that you claim we are. Instead, you decided to try to take matters into your own hands with some stupid plan that was never going to work, and I had to handle this." She gestured toward the body with a sigh.

"What did you do, Ainsley?" I couldn't decide whether to be horrified or impressed.

She rambled off what she'd done as if it were a grocery list. "I texted him after you fell asleep and told him to come here. Told him the deal was on. Then, after you left, I set up the room and waited. When he got here, I pretended to try to run, led him in here, and stabbed him."

"Wh-*what?* You should've told me what you were planning! I would've helped you. You have no idea how dangerous he is! He could've hurt you."

"Yeah, no kidding, but it's *you* who should've told *me!* And thank God I *did* have an idea how dangerous he was. Otherwise, I would've been left alone without a plan at all when he arrived."

"You're right," I admitted, nodding my head. "You're right. I should've told you. I just know how much you're dealing with right now with Maisy and the coach and... everything else. I was trying to take something off your plate and handle it myself."

"When will you realize I don't need to be protected? I just need to be on your team." She huffed a breath, setting her tea on the counter. "God, Peter, that's all I want. Why won't you let me in? What else do I have to do to prove to you that we're in this together?"

I stared down at the body between us, our biggest problem solved. She was right. She'd done enough—more than enough—to prove we were in this together. The gravity of the situation slammed into my chest. I could've lost her. She'd saved us. No thanks to me, she'd saved us.

"Nothing. I'm sorry. God, I'm sorry. You're...you're amazing, Ains. I'm so glad you're okay." I pulled her to me, kissing her. Suddenly, a passion of a new sort ignited in me. "You really did this?" I asked, pulling us apart and resting her forehead on mine.

"Mhm." She grinned wickedly. She'd enjoyed it. I could see that in her expression. *My little killer.*

"I want to hear every detail."

"Whatever you say." She kissed me again. "But let's take care of this first," she said, nodding toward the body. "We'll do it together."

"Good thinking." At least, one of us *was* thinking. All I could think of was her. "I'll get his head, you get his feet. Let's take him out back. I'll show you where to go."

At least for this part, she still needed me. This was where I excelled.

Without hesitation, we jumped into action, gripping his body in the tarp and dragging him down the hall. She'd wrapped the corners in duct tape, and I could see the blood pooling underneath the foggy plastic.

There was so much blood. It must've been a head injury.

Or an artery.

But which?

I wanted to know everything, but she was focused.

One thing at a time.

I kicked the back door open and we dragged him across the yard, completely hidden by the solace of our trees. We pulled the body past the garden and the fruit trees we'd planted when the kids were young.

When we'd reached the tree line, we were both panting and out of breath.

I couldn't believe this was happening.

It was like a fever dream.

For so long, I'd brought bodies to the woods alone, buried them alone, reveled in these moments alone. I thought bringing Ainsley into the process would take some of the enjoyment out of it for me, but as I stared at her, panting and sweaty, flecks of blood in her hair and eyelashes, knowing what she'd done... I could only wonder why I hadn't brought her into my world sooner.

There were two versions of myself. The version I showed the world: the father, the architect, the husband, the friend. Then there was the version that existed underneath all of that, the one only my victims, Jim, and now my wife knew: animalistic, vengeful, insatiable.

Seeing her come into that world, come to know that version, had once repulsed me. Terrified me.

Now I couldn't think of anything more natural.

Of course she should know me in this state.

The protector.

The animal.

Stripped down to my basic, primal needs.

Her being one of them.

Maybe this was the solution to my desires, after all. Maybe she was right.

She swiped her hand across her forehead. "Where to?"

She needed me here. She was helpless for the next part. She couldn't dig the graves, couldn't bury the bodies.

She needed me.

She needed me.

She needed me.

"Peter," she said, her tone pointed, and I snapped out of my thoughts.

"Sorry. This way." I jutted my head to our left and led her down the small path and past the gully. We went down one side and up the other, stopping occasionally to catch our breath.

"How much farther?" she asked when we stopped the final time between two large oak trees.

"It's here," I told her, wiping sweat from my upper lip.

"Here?" Her eyes widened, staring at the ground below her. She was standing just above the bodies I'd buried, though you couldn't tell at a glance. I'd been careful, meticulous about their placement, making sure to keep the ground as undisturbed as possible.

I came back occasionally, even when I didn't need to, just to check on them.

They were my trophies.

The pairs of underwear were one thing, but the bodies, those were the true prizes.

My victims were the only ones who knew what I was capable of.

At least, until now.

"I'll go get a shovel from the garage," she said, turning

and rushing back toward the house. I nodded, then bent down, pulling back a bit of the tarp to look at his face.

Even through the plastic, I could see the dark, black line running across his neck. I grinned.

It wasn't a method I would've chosen, but it worked.

It got the job done.

I replaced the tarp, covering his face again.

Jim didn't deserve to be buried with my victims—he wasn't special enough. He'd tried to harm Ainsley. But I owed him thanks for introducing me to the darkest, most satisfying parts of myself. For that, he would be buried with respect, albeit separately.

After several minutes had passed, Ainsley returned with two shovels and we set to work, digging carefully closest to the oak tree on the left.

"Are the others close by?" she asked cautiously.

"Close, yeah." I wanted to tell her everything, but I couldn't. Something inside of me prevented it, as much as I loved this. That was before, this was now. She could know everything going forward, but those memories were just mine.

I needed to retain control of them.

To my relief, she continued digging without asking anything else.

It was grueling work, especially in the summer heat, but it would all be worth it. I measured the hole with the length of my shovel. Once it was large enough to fit the entire thing, I tossed the shovel aside.

"Okay, slide him to me slowly," I instructed, easing down inside the grave. She leaned forward, pushing his body forward, her breasts pressing against the top of her tank top. I shook my head, trying to focus. It was a struggle, though. This was a whole new level of excitement for me. The two things I loved most in the world combined into one moment. One fleeting, intense, powerful moment that would be over all too soon.

Once the body was inside the grave, we shoveled the dirt on top of him. We started slowly, making sure we'd covered every inch of him, then began to push the dirt in quicker.

Goodbye, old friend.

If someone had told me years ago that our friendship, the one that started the day I moved into my dorm room all those years ago, would end with him being buried in my backyard, I never would've believed it.

But this was how it had to happen. He'd gotten in over his head, pushed us too far. That was the problem with Jim—he didn't know how to take no for an answer. He always wanted something more.

With the last of the dirt shoveled over top of him, I stepped onto the grave, stamping it down. I held out a hand for Ainsley and she joined me, stepping onto fresh dirt cautiously.

"Help me even it out."

Once the earth was flattened as much as possible, she stepped off the grave, swiping the back of her hand across her forehead and reaching for the shovel.

"We really should've brought water out here. It's scorching."

I couldn't listen, couldn't respond. The version of myself she had yet to meet was still here, still in control. I grabbed her arm, my grip too tight, and she turned her head to look at me.

"What are you—"

I cupped her face, pressing our lips together and forcing her backward until we smacked into the tree. She whimpered, but I didn't care.

Couldn't.

Pain was necessary sometimes.

Our kisses were hot and feverish, moans of pure ecstasy escaping our throats as I pulled her shirt over her head, breaking apart for merely a second.

God, she was beautiful.

I gripped her hands together, holding them above her head against the tree. I trailed passionate kisses across her collarbone, tasting the saltiness of her skin.

I lifted my face to hers, rubbing the stubble on my chin across her cheek as I moved toward her ear. "Tell me what you did to him."

Her eyes widened with shock, then narrowed as she tried to pull away from me. We locked eyes, a challenge in mine. "Tell me."

Dark heat filled her expression. "I killed him."

I lowered my mouth to her breast, biting at a bit of her flesh. She jolted. "Tell me how."

I closed my mouth over her breast, tempting and teasing her. She moaned, her eyes closed with pleasure, mouth dropped open. When she didn't say anything, I stopped and released her hands, pulling her face to look at me with force. *"Tell. Me. How."* I slipped my hand inside her pants, my fingers between her legs as she twisted and writhed against me. I pressed my forehead to hers, her breath on my lips. She tried to kiss me, but I held back. *"Tell. Me. How."* I removed my hand from between her legs, refusing to do anything else until she'd answered me. "Ainsley, now. Tell me!"

"With...with a knife." She panted. "Please, Peter..."

"Good girl." I rewarded her, slipping my fingers back in place. "Did he beg you to stop?"

She bit her bottom lip, shaking her head.

"No? Say it. Tell me."

"No." Her voice was breathless. I removed my hand, much to her disapproval. "Don't stop..."

Heat shot through me like lightning as I pulled away from her and slid her pants down her legs, each inch of skin exposed met with a kiss. I tossed them across the woods, far from us. I wanted to see all of her.

It was what Jim had wanted.

What everyone wanted when they saw her.

But she was only mine.

Forever.

I kneeled in front of her, taking in the sight of her innocent eyes watching me. Waiting. Wondering what I was going to do. "Did he know it was coming?"

"No," she said, gripping my hair with both hands, trying to force me toward her. I stayed strong.

I was stronger than her, and I wanted to remind her of that. I let her continue to try, though, hardly wavering in place, even with the pain as she pulled my hair harder. I could feel nothing but desire at that moment.

Nothing but want.

"No?"

"I caught him by surprise," she said breathlessly.

"How did he look? After you'd done it?" I asked, grabbing her hands from the top of my head and pushing them against the tree. "Scared?"

"Terrified." She bit her lip again, and I leaned forward, giving in and pressing my mouth exactly where she wanted it. To the place that belonged only to me.

She cried out and I stood, unable to control myself any longer. I grabbed her, spinning her around and shoving her body into the tree. She was shaking, pressing up on her toes as I unhooked my pants and entered her from behind, white-hot pleasure ricocheting through me.

She cried out again, and I covered her mouth with my hand, wanting her quieter and louder at the same time. I pressed my face to her hair, breathing in her scent as we moved together, perfectly in sync.

It was funny.

Once, I'd thought I could only feel this way when ending a life, but here it was with her...that inexplicable feeling I'd spent my life chasing. I couldn't put my finger on exactly what it was.

I felt...

Free.

Awake.

Alive.

Yes, maybe that was it.

I'd never... Never felt so alive.

CHAPTER TWENTY-ONE

AINSLEY

It was as if a switch had flipped in my husband. Similar to how things had changed between us after Stefan, suddenly we were better.

The honeymoon stage had reappeared; the light was back in his eyes.

This time, though, there was a hunger, a darkness to him I hadn't seen before. The power I felt at ending Jim's life was nothing compared to the power I saw in his expression when he looked at me.

I couldn't help feeling like I was someone else entirely to him now.

I wanted to hold on to that.

For so long, I'd struggled to get him to look at me the way he was looking at me now. I'd caught glimpses of it before, but this was a full, unobstructed view.

I wanted to capture it, bottle it, whatever it took to make sure it remained mine forever.

Peter had told me once that after you'd ended your first life, each one got easier.

I understood that with Stefan, and then Jim.

The shock wore off quicker, replaced by magnetic intensity.

The next day, as I left the house, I felt the pull. Already, I wanted to do it again.

How did Peter manage to control himself?

I was starting to wonder if I ever would again.

Or if I even wanted to.

Last night, we'd cleaned up what little mess there was, bleached our clothes, and loaded the boxes up into the back of Jim's truck. We'd taken the body Jim had left with us and buried her far from the other victims. I was sore and exhausted, but I'd hardly slept at all. It was invigorating. I could keep going—living on this high forever. My body was on fire with electricity like I'd never felt before. I wanted to sit with it, to absorb it and let it linger, but I had to return to my life. I knew that. If this was ever going to work, I had to keep up pretenses.

So, we'd come up with a plan. Peter had hidden Jim's truck at the edge of our property before the kids got home so they wouldn't notice it. This morning, he'd left before they were up to take the boxes to the landfill, then I was supposed to meet him near a hiking trail without much traffic and we'd leave Jim's truck there.

I'd been worried about who might come looking for him, but Peter assured me no one was going to look for Jim Slater.

He was a loner.

A rapist.

A felon.

A murderer.

An all-around bad guy.

The world was a better place without him. Thanks to me.

I'd told my team I had a few errands to run—which was technically true—and I'd be a few hours late to work. As I drove the streets on my way to find Peter, a bit of doubt began to creep in. I tried not to let it get to me, not to stress over what might come next.

There were things I couldn't control, and that was okay. I'd learn to live with it.

Things were good now.

I'd protected Peter from his enemy. Protected our family. Protected the world.

I am the whole damn world.

I repeated the mantra over and over in my head. It made me feel powerful. More powerful than I'd ever felt.

I understood the hype.

The addiction.

The excitement.

For the first time in my life, I felt like I understood my husband completely.

FIVE MINUTES earlier than we'd planned, I slowed the car next to the place where we were supposed to meet. He wasn't there yet, but he was coming. We had more work to do, and we weren't wasting any time.

Next up was Coach Chris and, if it was possible, I was even more excited about killing him.

It wasn't smart to murder them so close together, but we both agreed this was a special circumstance. We couldn't let him go on living. Couldn't chance him hurting someone else.

I thought about Bailey, the young girl who'd grown up with Maisy. Who'd spent the night at our house countless times. Who'd worn matching clothes with Maisy when they were younger. Whose voice I could still hear blaring through the walls on the old karaoke machine Maisy had been gifted for Christmas when they were seven.

We'd agreed turning him in would only hurt Maisy worse. Perhaps cost her a cherished friendship.

So, if we couldn't go to the police, murder was our only option.

Or...maybe that's just what we wanted to believe. Either way, it was what would be done.

I spied Jim's truck headed in my direction, slowing down as it neared me. Peter wore Jim's ball cap, and when he got close, he lifted it slightly, flashing a boy-like grin at me and pulling down the path and into the woods until the truck was hidden from passing cars.

"Did you have any trouble?" I asked, coming to join him as he wiped down the inside of the truck and the door handles.

"Nothing I couldn't handle."

"You paid in cash, right?"

"Yep."

"Good."

I must've sounded nervous because he looked at me over his shoulder, nodding slowly. "We're fine. Trust me, no one's going to be looking for him. I've told the partners he's pulling all his contracts. We're replacing him at work. None of his employees will be shocked. And there's no one else. His parents cut him off years ago, he has no friends... We're fine."

I nodded, swallowing hard. "I know."

The roles had reversed so much from the last time, when it had been me reassuring him. Once the truck had been wiped down, we crossed the woods back to our car.

"To the studio?"

I nodded as we buckled in. "It's a few hours before practices will start, so he should be there alone."

"And if he's not?"

"We'll figure that out if it comes to it." I gripped the steering wheel tightly, reversing out of the parking spot and turning our car in the direction we were headed.

"How did the kids seem? Were they awake before you left?"

"Dylan and Riley are fine. I mean, normal, but fine. Maisy still isn't really talking to me."

"She'll come around."

"I don't know, Peter. I really butchered this," I said, shaking my head.

"What are you talking about?"

"She needed me to be there for her, to say the right thing, and I just...didn't. I was rambling about turning him in and I wasn't listening to her. To what she needed."

"You were shocked." He reached for my hand, and I gave it to him, though it did little to reassure me.

"That's no excuse."

"You did all you could. You listened to her—"

"Yeah, and that's all I should've done. For all we know, she'll never tell me anything again."

"That's not true."

"You don't know that—"

"I do," he said firmly. "Ains, you love her. She knows that."

"But is that enough? When I just keep failing her?"

"You're not failing her. She'll never know that you did this, of course, but you'll know. You're protecting her now. Just like you always have. She'll see that someday. No, maybe you didn't do exactly what you hoped in that moment, but what you said was what any other parent would've said. It's what *I* would've said."

Somehow, that did little to make me feel better.

"Anyway, let's just focus, okay? Should we go over the plan one more time?"

We did—rehearsing and rerunning the plan over and over as we made our way toward the tiny dance studio at the edge of town. To my relief, only one car was there when we arrived. The forest green hatchback was parked on the far side of the lot, leaving room for the parents who would arrive this evening.

"You ready?" he asked, eyeing me from the passenger seat.

I pushed open the door and stepped out. "As I'll ever be."

"Be careful."

I shut the door, leaving him waiting in the car, and closed my hands into fists, breathing deeply as I counted my steps on the way to the door.

Calm down.

Calm down.

Calm down.

I tugged at the shirt I was wearing, lowering my neckline and praying it would work in my favor. No amount of preparation could've made this easier. Not when there were so many variables. It was easier at home, but this couldn't be done at home.

It just couldn't. There was no way to get the coach to our house without seeming suspicious.

I wore a ball cap, though there were no cameras in the studio. It had never seemed odd to me before, though now I had to suspect Coach being cheap wasn't the only reason for that.

I opened the glass door, the bell above it chiming to announce my presence, and listened for his footsteps. His office was just down the hall and to the left.

I moved slowly, heading down the dark corridor and toward the door I'd entered so many times before—to pay tuition or purchase the newest costume.

Once I'd reached it, I placed my hand on the small silver handle and pulled without warning, easing my head inside.

Coach was at his desk, his brow furrowed as he stared intently at something on the computer. When he saw me, he glanced up, then did a double take. "Ainsley? Hey, whoa. I didn't hear you come in." He checked his watch. "Was I expecting you?"

Clearing his throat, he closed out of whatever was on his screen, then stood.

"No," I said softly. "Sorry to interrupt. Is this a bad time?"

"Not at all." He gestured toward the chairs in front of his desk. "Come on in. It's great to see you."

My smile felt more like a grimace, but I knew it would

look dazzling to him. That was my superpower, after all, and the reason I'd been the one to come inside. I could hide my emotions—my rage—like Peter never could.

"So, this is kind of embarrassing, but I'm actually here because I just discovered Maisy had dropped dance."

His resolve disappeared for a half second, but like a pro himself, he managed to disguise it. He blinked rapidly, clearing his throat again. "Um, you did?" His nervous laugh grated my nerves. "Yeah, she dropped...last season, I guess. I assumed you knew?"

"I didn't," I said, clasping my hands in my lap. I dug my nails into my palms, trying to remain still when all I wanted to do was lunge across the desk and claw his eyeballs out with my bare hands. "Did she tell you why she dropped out? She's always loved dancing so much. It's quite a shock to us, as you can imagine."

The color drained from his face. "I, well, yeah... It was a shock to me, too. She was one of my stars. But I had to respect her choice. She didn't really give me an answer. I can try to talk to her, if you want."

"No," I said too quickly, then repeated it in a soft, slow croon. "*No.* I'll take care of that. You're *so* busy, I mean." I batted my eyelashes at him, leaning forward and sticking out my chest, though he hardly seemed to notice. In fact, he scooted back in his chair, farther away from me. Perhaps I was too old for his tastes.

"Well, I'd love to have her back here. We miss her."

"She mentioned a lot of her friends had quit, too. Bailey and Jennessa... Any idea about them?"

Beads of sweat had begun forming on his upper lip. He shook his head, forcing a charming, albeit terrified, grin.

"No. Nope. I never really got an answer. You know how young girls are..."

"How *are* they?" I asked, unable to control myself. The condescending tone of his voice was nails on a chalkboard.

"Hm?" His brows shot up.

"Well, I mean, to be frank, I'd assume you'd know."

He adjusted in his chair, tugging at his pant legs as he released a nervous laugh. "What do you mean?"

"Well, I just mean you work with them all day, after all."

"Oh, right." He glanced at the floor. "Yeah. Sorry..." He paused, drawing in a breath. For a moment, we were quiet and he patted his legs awkwardly, looking around the room. "Hey, was there something else I could help you with? I forgot I actually do have a meeting to get to after this."

A meeting. I scoffed internally, pushing up from my chair.

"Of course. I don't want to take up too much of your time. I just wanted to ask you about one more thing."

"Sure." He stood, too.

I reached into my pocket, pulling out my phone.

He leaned forward as I scrolled through my photos, searching for the one I'd found on Maisy's phone the night before after she'd fallen asleep.

I couldn't blame Maisy for lying to me about the things he'd sent her. From what I could see, the conversations had been mainly one sided, but still, I would've been mortified to tell my mother what happened, too.

"Ah, here it is. Can you tell me... Is this yours?" I flashed the screen at him.

"What the hell?" As he leaned in, I slipped the syringe out of my sleeve and plunged it into his neck. He staggered backward, a hand pressed to the injection site, his eyes wide. I had to hope it worked as quickly as the Internet said it would. "What the hell?" he repeated. "What did you do?" He took a wobbly step toward me, but froze, staring up at the ceiling and blinking rapidly.

I grinned.

It was working.

When going through the boxes Jim had left behind, we'd come across several filled with vials of a clear substance. On a whim, we'd searched for their uses using his phone—couldn't have anything traced back to us, after all—and were pleasantly surprised to find out that the vials held a particularly nasty sedative.

It was all that we'd kept from Jim's many packages, but, as luck would have it, it was all we'd need. From what we'd read, just a drop could tranquilize an elephant.

I'd guessed on the dosage.

"I can...explain..." His words came out garbled, as if he were choking. He didn't need to say a word. The confession was in his mortified expression. I didn't need any further proof—I'd seen it all on her phone—but I wanted him to know I knew. Wanted him to understand why this was happening.

"It's okay. I think I get the picture. Pun intended." I wrinkled my nose at him playfully.

"You've...got it all wrong." He checked his palm, then placed it back on the injection site, gripping the desk to keep from collapsing. "What did you do? What did you give me? I'm calling the police." He reached for the top drawer, pulling it open and tumbling sideways.

"Go right ahead. I have plenty of pictures and text messages to show them. You'd actually be saving me a phone call."

"No, you've gotta believe me... It's a misunderst—" He blinked again, cutting himself off, one hand on his head. "I have no idea where you got that, but I swear to you... It's... It's not me!"

I stepped back, sliding my phone into my pocket as he fought to stand up, leaning his full weight on the book-shelf behind his desk. It wouldn't be long now.

I pulled the knife from my pocket, pointing it directly between his legs.

"That'll be easy enough to prove, considering the disgusting birthmark on your leg."

He eyed the knife, still in disbelief. "Those things can be...edited. Come on, Ainsley. You... You know me. You know how much I love these girls," he pleaded.

"Oh, yes. I know all about that."

"I'm not capable of this."

"It's a funny thing. What people are capable of. They always manage to surprise you."

He stood again, his arms and legs out wide, trying to prevent himself from toppling over. "I don't feel good... Seriously, what did you give me?"

"Not much time now. Better find somewhere soft to land."

"Wha—"

Before he could finish the question, his knees gave out

and he dropped to the floor, his head hitting the hardwood with a loud thud.

I huffed out a sigh and stood over him, watching him breathe. I could've killed him right then—I wanted to, even—but that wasn't the plan. I slipped the knife back into my pocket and adjusted the cap, turning back toward the door to get Peter's help. I stopped short, gasping when I heard a noise behind me.

Was he waking up? I'd given him enough sedative to kill him, or knock him out for days at the very least.

Buzzz...

Buzzz...

Buzzz...

I spun back around. The sound was coming from inside his desk. Pulling my sleeves over my hands, I stepped over him and peered inside the top drawer he'd torn open. His phone lay faceup, a woman's portrait and name on the screen.

Joanna.

A dance mom, perhaps?

She was pretty. Too old for his taste, maybe, but... My eyes trailed the length of his desk, noticing the pictures I'd never seen before. The same woman who was on his screen was in the pictures. They were smiling, gazing at each other with warm, loving stares. In the next picture, their arms wrapped around each other, their lips locked together.

They seemed happy.

In love.

Didn't she know what a monster he was?

Joanna...

Coach wasn't married. Was this a new girlfriend? A fiancée?

Fuck.

I slammed the drawer shut, trying to think.

Coach was one thing—he deserved it. But we'd believed he was single, just like Jim. There wasn't supposed to be anyone who'd really be looking for him. A simple text saying he was going out of town for a while was going to solve this. The assistant coaches could pick up his slack and no one was meant to miss him.

Would Joanna complicate that plan?

It didn't matter, really. There was no going back.

Sorry, Joanna. Your boyfriend sucks.

CHAPTER TWENTY-TWO

PETER

PRESENT DAY

The therapist needed to die.

I didn't understand why Ainsley couldn't see that. She was a liability. We'd gone to see her with the understanding that we were scoping her out, trying to learn what we could about her before we eventually killed her.

It was unfortunate, but necessary.

We booked our session under the guise of needing couple's therapy, but we were just biding our time.

Coach Chris had disappeared just a month earlier, and so far, no one seemed to be questioning it too much.

But the fact that he had a girlfriend—from what we could tell, that's all she was—meant eventually, she would start asking questions that would get the police's attention. If we could take her out before then, it would save us all the headache.

It was why we'd gotten off so easily with Jim, but

Stefan's disappearance had caused a full-on investigation. With my personal victims, I'd never had any true connection to them, and there was nothing to lead the police to me, but with Chris, all the evidence they'd need could surely be found if they only looked hard enough.

I didn't regret it—not even slightly.

I'd do it a million times over, even knowing I was going to jail if it meant protecting Maisy from this predator. But still, if I had a choice, obviously not being found out was my preference.

That was why I went back to see Joanna St. James alone a few days after our first joint session. I wanted to know more about her, and fast.

She walked out of her office and saw me sitting on her couch.

Waiting for her.

She recognized me; I saw it in her eyes. She smiled with a warmth that reminded me of Christmas morning. There was a real beauty to her—something special. Something I couldn't fully appreciate when Ainsley was there.

"Pete." My name was a full sentence on her lips, without having to consult her schedule. She knew me. She was happy to see me. "I wasn't expecting you back so soon. Is everything okay?"

"Yeah," I said. Cool. Casual. I stood, extending my hand. "Sorry to drop in like this." I gestured toward her secretary. "Taylor said you had an opening, and I thought I'd try to get a one-on-one session. I mean, if that's okay?"

"Of course it is." She pushed open the door to her office and allowed me to walk past her. As I did, I inhaled the scent of her. Clean, like soap and a light lotion. Not too much. Just enough.

I liked that.

She shut the door behind her and I sank down onto the couch where Ainsley and I had sat during our session.

"So, what can I do for you, Pete?" I liked the way my name sounded coming out of her mouth. She sat down across from me. She was more comfortable today. Happier. Because it was just us.

No distractions.

She leaned back on the couch, elbow bent on the arm of it so she could rest her head on her fist.

"Well, I just thought…as much as I agree we need couple's therapy, Annie and I both have issues to work on by ourselves, too." I bobbed my head sideways, admitting, "Her more than me, maybe."

She didn't smile at my joke.

"Anyway…" I cleared my throat. "I thought if I started coming for private sessions, I could convince her to do the same."

"I see…" She adjusted her skirt, and I couldn't help but think she wanted me to notice her legs. "Well, I'm happy to help you however I can. But I do think it's important that you communicate with Annie the fact that you're doing these sessions."

"Of course," I assured her.

"Okay, great. Should we get started then?"

She liked when I told her what to do.

"Yes. I'd like that."

She smiled.

She'd liked that, too.

CHAPTER TWENTY-THREE

AINSLEY

I pulled up outside Joanna's office a week after our first session. We'd agreed not to go back—not wanting to be seen and remembered by her secretary—but I couldn't resist the urge to see her again.

Peter was ready to kill her. To take her out and be done with it all, but I just wasn't.

Meeting her had changed my mind.

I could never explain it to my husband, but in the strangest way, I felt as if Joanna was me.

With a twist of fate, I could've been her. If one of the husbands, boyfriends, or fathers of any of his victims had killed my husband, I'd be the woman left behind.

The liability.

Perhaps they would've killed me simply for loving him.

Even if I was oblivious to his crimes.

Was Joanna oblivious? Surely she didn't know what he was doing. Not to children... She was a therapist. Of all people, she understood the ramifications.

It was why I needed to go back. To look her in the eye without Peter there, to talk to her honestly and try to get a better read on who she was as a person.

"Annie?" The door to her office opened, and she stepped out, her eyes washing over me. "I'm so glad you could come." Her smile seemed so genuine I wanted to believe her.

Then again, it was her job to make me believe her, wasn't it?

How many of her clients did she actually like?

How many did she dread seeing?

I stood, following her lead as she ushered me into the office. "Thanks for fitting me into your schedule. You're probably wondering why I'm here alone..." I sat on the sofa and watched as she moved to sit in front of me, her brows knitted together with apparent confusion. "The truth is, I think I might see more benefit from coming to see you by myself than if Pete and I came together."

"I see..." She studied me.

"He's not really big on therapy, as I'm sure you could tell, but I think you might be able to help me, even if I can't get him back."

She nodded slowly, obviously processing the fact that we weren't coming back. "What is it you need help with?"

Suddenly, I felt as if I'd overstepped. "Is this okay?" I moved to stand. "If this is out of line, just let me know. You've already met the two of us. I can understand if it's against the rules for you to see me separat—"

"Annie, sit," she said, holding a hand out. "You aren't breaking any rules. I'm glad you're here."

Whether or not it was true, I wanted to believe it.

"Thank you." I breathed a sigh of relief. "I'm sorry I'm such a mess. This is kind of overwhelming, you know?"

She gave a nod. "What's overwhelming?"

"All of this. I mean, I wanted to see you with Pete, but he won't come with me. He says he doesn't think you can help." I corrected myself. "Not *you*, specifically. Just therapy in general." Inhaling deeply, I leaned over my knees. "I'm sorry, can we start over?"

"Just breathe, Annie…" She instructed, her tone soothing. "Just take a breath. Let's start out with why you think you're here."

I nodded. *That* I could answer. "I'm here because… sometimes I think I can't trust my husband. And I'm not sure if that's a *him* problem or a *me* problem."

"Okay. And what specifically are you struggling to trust him with? Has he been unfaithful?"

I looked away, unsure how to answer that question. Of course he'd been unfaithful. Once when he'd had permission to be, but countless other times, too. The problem was, it wasn't the infidelity that bothered me. Not really. It was everything else.

"No. Not really."

She waited for me to say more.

"This is a safe space. Whatever you say here, you can trust that I won't say a word to Pete."

I rested my head in my palms. It had been so long since I felt safe. Perhaps I was only realizing that for the first time right then. What I'd mistaken as safety with Peter hadn't felt like this.

Here, I was in a cocoon.

Home felt like a web.

"Pete's not unfaithful, but he's obsessive…"

"Over you?"

"No. Over his hobbies."

"Fencing," she filled in, obviously remembering the subject that had taken up so much of our time during the couple's session.

"Right."

"And that makes you feel lonely."

"He won't let me do it with him. I mean, there've been a few times. And when we do, it's really good. Great, actually. It's like, that's the only time we can connect."

"When you fence?"

If she thought it was odd, she wasn't letting on.

"Right, but it's like he gets possessive over it. He won't let me all the way in."

She tilted her head to the side slightly. It was rare to talk to someone who really cared to listen. Joanna was that kind of person, even if it was only because she was being paid. "Tell me, does Pete involve himself in your hobbies? Does he make an effort to do the things you enjoy?"

What did I enjoy? Truth was, I had no idea anymore.

"Not really, no."

"Do you invite him to join you?"

I chewed my bottom lip. "I don't really have hobbies."

"Everybody has hobbies…"

"My best friend, Glennon, she's the one who spends time with me when I just need to relax. But we don't really do anything. Just watch trashy TV and snack, usually."

"A woman after my own heart." She smiled. So, we

were alike. "And how does Pete feel about that? About Glennon being the person you go to when you need to relax?"

"Pete and Glennon have a"—I fought to suppress a grin —"complicated relationship."

"I see."

"I mean, they're fine. It's just a long, sordid history."

She nodded, picking up the pen and blank notepad from the table in front of her. "Okay, so let's go back a bit. Tell me about when you first met Pete. What attracted you to him?"

"We were in college…" I started in on the story, settling into the part of our past I was incredibly comfortable with.

The safe part.

The cozy part.

Before the fencing.

Before everything changed.

CHAPTER TWENTY-FOUR

PETER

"Where do you think your problems with Annie come from, Pete?" she asked, watching me closely.

It was our second session alone, and I still hadn't gotten over how much I liked having her eyes on me.

"I love her," I said, like a good husband. "But I hate feeling like she's always trying to control me. I mean, sometimes I don't mind it. You know, my parents were all over the place when I was growing up. I have three older brothers, and my house was always loud and obnoxious. People were always screaming and fighting. When I met Annie, she was so...calm." I thought for a moment, then corrected myself. "Calm isn't the right word. She's like a storm you can see from a distance. I always know something's brewing with her, but she doesn't ever get close enough to feel the rain. Does that make sense?"

She didn't answer, just kept watching me. She'd been fidgeting with the pen a lot more today. I was making her nervous.

"To a certain extent, she makes me feel..." I searched for a manlier word than *safe.* "Like everything's under control. After a lifetime of feeling like nothing's in control, Annie gives me peace. I can drop the ball and know that she's always going to be there to pick it up. There are hardly any fights in our house. It's safe. Quiet. Our kids are well-rounded. Loved. It's the opposite of what I experienced growing up. She's the opposite of my mother."

"You have a bad relationship with your mother?"

"My father was wild—always running around, cheating on her, drinking, partying. My brothers were the same. So, most of the time, it was just me and Mom at home. She blamed it all on me. I was the youngest, so I was easy enough to pick on. I had rules no one else had to follow. I had to keep the house in order." I cleared my throat. "We haven't spoken in years."

"Some of what you've told me about Annie, though, the way she treats you... Does she remind you of your mother at all? You said there was no control in your house, but it sounds like your mother tried to control everyone by controlling you. Is that accurate?"

I'd never thought about it that way, but maybe she was right. Maybe that's why Ainsley had always been different for me.

Why I could never hurt her.

Why I could never hurt my mother. Even when I'd had the chance.

"It could be."

Ainsley had told me once that she tried to control us

because to her, that felt like love. Maybe *being* controlled felt like love to me.

God, we certainly were a match, weren't we?

After a moment, Joanna went on. "Do you ever think maybe that's why you want to…to fence alone? Because it's the one small thing that still belongs exclusively to you? The one thing no one else controls? Not Annie? Not your mother?"

It felt true, even if I'd never been able to put it into those words. "Maybe, yeah."

"Do you find yourself turning to fencing when you've had a particularly bad day? Maybe when you've had a fight with Annie or something went wrong at work?"

I nodded.

Damn, she was good.

"And how does Annie react to that?"

"At first, I didn't know she knew what I was doing. I kept it hidden."

"But when she found out?"

"She was…well, she wanted to be involved."

"Why do you think that was?"

I shrugged. "You tell me. You're the expert." I locked eyes with her, lingering in the moment as her cheeks flushed pink. She recovered quickly, but not before I'd mentally saved the image.

I could use that later.

"Well, we know Annie isn't the type of person who actually enjoys fencing…"

Annie doesn't belong here, Joanna. It's just you and me.

Soon enough, I'd convince her to talk about us instead. For now, I shook my head. "Not particularly."

She smiled as if we'd just had a breakthrough, though I wasn't sure I understood it. "So maybe you actually enjoy having more control than you think, and maybe Annie enjoys seeing you *out* of her control more than she thinks. The two of you are fighting against your inner nature and trying to achieve opposite things, when you really want the same thing—you're trying to let her control you and she's trying to control you, all the while, you're happiest when you have a bit of that control back and she's happiest when you take it back. Do you see what I'm saying?"

I nodded, though she'd completely lost me.

"So, you're saying I should put my foot down about fencing?"

"I'm saying you should do what feels right to you, and I think Annie will appreciate you being honest with her. But you can't push her out. You have to tell her why it's important to you. Let go of who you think you're supposed to be and just accept who you are." She saw me for me. I knew that. Joanna had always seen me for who I was. She understood me like no one else. "Communication is where you're lacking. Both of you."

"Communication," I repeated. She wore a satisfied grin that had my mind spinning. "You're a genius."

"I don't know about that," she said with a laugh. "You're doing all the work. I'm just helping you connect the pieces." She liked helping me just about as much as I liked having her help me.

She glanced at the clock, and I felt a dull ache in my core. It meant it was almost time to leave her. For another week. I wasn't sure if I could do it.

Seven days felt like torture when all I wanted to do was see her again. Through the open window to our left, I could see the parking lot where my car was waiting. It would be painful to walk back to it without her.

"One more thing," she said, interrupting my thoughts and leaning forward over her knees.

I leaned forward, too, as close as I could get to her. I could smell her scent again. I needed to find out what soap it was and stock up on it. How could I ask her without coming off creepy?

"Fencing," she said, wrinkling her nose. "It's not really *fencing*, is it?"

My blood ran cold.

Well, shit.

CHAPTER TWENTY-FIVE

AINSLEY

I sat across from Joanna with a mug of tea in my hand. I was restless that day.

I couldn't put Peter off much longer.

He hadn't brought it up in a few days, but I knew he wanted to go back to see her. To kill her. After our couple's session, he kept saying we needed to put an end to her before she went to the police.

I had no idea how to explain to him why I couldn't. I couldn't tell him the truth. That she was me. That we were the same.

I could never tell him about our sessions, or how it genuinely felt like maybe she was helping me.

I was back for my third session, and they'd already begun to feel like a much-needed reprieve.

I wasn't sure I could make it without Joanna anymore.

I couldn't let Peter take her from me.

"Are you married, Joanna?" I asked, glancing over at her from where I sat.

She looked taken aback. "Um, no. We really shouldn't be talking about that, Annie. This is about you."

Because we weren't friends. I had to remember that.

She was my therapist.

That was it.

"You just have so much insight into all of this. You must have someone."

"Well, actually, I do have a boyfriend," she said finally. "He's been out of town, but he'll be back soon. He's supposed to be coming to my house when he gets into town."

"When will that be?"

"This weekend," she lied. "Maybe sooner."

"That'll be nice," I told her. She had no reason to lie to me. Her boyfriend's body was currently decaying several feet from where I slept at night. Still, I didn't press the issue.

Back to business. I sucked in a breath, picking at the skin around my finger. "Tell me the truth. Is it crazy to still want to be with my husband? After everything? The lies? The sneaking around? Are we just bad for each other?"

She seemed to contemplate my questions, a flicker of fear in her eyes. I'd told her too much, perhaps. I think she was starting to worry. She chose her words carefully. "I think sometimes people show us who they are, and we have to choose whether or not we're going to believe them. There's personality, Annie, and there's human nature. Some things can be changed. Some people can change. But some things, some things are so deep down at the core of who we are, no matter what the people around

182

us do, nothing will change us. If Pete has shown you who he is, you have to decide if you can live with it. If he's unwilling to change, you have to decide if *you're* going to change. Because if you're both unhappy, one of you has to."

I nodded slowly. It wasn't what I wanted to hear, but it was what I was slowly starting to understand.

My eyes flicked up to the clock on the wall, realizing how much time had passed. Peter would be getting ready to leave the office, and I needed to head out.

"I should go."

She started to protest—we had so much more to talk about and I was cutting our time short—but I needed to go. I had too much swimming through my head. I needed time to process it all before I saw my husband.

I WAS in the kitchen later when Maisy and Bailey walked in the door, laughing about a joke I hadn't heard.

"Hey, Mom. How was work?"

"Work was work," I said. "Did I tell you Tara's having a baby?"

Maisy's eyes lit up. "She is? No way! When is she due?"

"Well, she just found out a few weeks ago, so she's very early still. She's due sometime next summer. She brought in a sonogram today." I pulled out my phone and showed her the photograph I'd snapped. "See that tiny white speck? That's the baby."

"Awww... It's so little."

I closed my phone. "Hey, do you think I could talk to you for a second?"

Maisy looked at Bailey hesitantly. "Uh… About what?"

"It'll just take a second. Bailey, I made that tray of snacks for you girls. Why don't you carry it to the bedroom?"

She paused with a worried glance toward Maisy, but finally agreed. "Sure thing, Mrs. G." She lifted the tray of veggies and hummus and carried it down the hall. Once I'd heard the door shut, I turned to my daughter.

"I just wanted to check in and see how everything's going at school. Is Bailey staying away from Coach?"

I hadn't mentioned it once since she'd told me that day at the lake, and she seemed grateful not to have to discuss it, so I worried about her reaction. But to my relief, she said, "Oh. Actually, Coach left."

"Left?" I raised my brows, feigning surprise.

"He, like, moved or something. A few girls from the team said Ashley and Eleanor have been coaching for, like, a month now. They said he'd be coming back, but he hasn't." She shrugged one shoulder.

"And Bailey hasn't heard from him? You're not going to get into trouble. I promised you I wouldn't say anything, and I haven't."

"No, Mom, I swear. She hasn't heard from him. I would tell you."

"Okay," I said hesitantly. "You know I just want to protect you both."

She nodded, jutting a thumb over her shoulder. "Can I go now?"

"Yep, go have fun."

She turned to walk away, but stopped. "Hey, Mom?"

"Yeah?"

"Thanks for...you know, being cool about everything."

I clutched my chest in mock surprise. "Can I get you to repeat that so I can record it?"

She groaned playfully. "Well, don't ruin it now."

I giggled. "You know you can tell me anything, kiddo. I mean that."

"I know."

Heavy footsteps sounded down the hall, interrupting our moment, and I stepped forward to see Peter coming up the stairs. He headed for the bedroom just as Maisy darted off, disappearing into her own room.

I followed Peter, opening the bedroom door slowly.

He froze, but looked relieved when he saw me. "Hey, beautiful." He'd been in good spirits lately, though the initial thrills from both Jim and Chris had worn off entirely too fast.

"How was work?"

"Busy. Exhausting." He flopped onto the bed as if to prove a point. "How was your day?"

"My day was busy, too. Tara's having a baby."

"Is she? Nice." He folded his hands across his forehead, closing his eyes.

"Hey, I've been thinking..." I trailed a hand across his chest.

"Yeah?" One eye popped open.

"What do you say we pick someone new?"

"Someone new?" Now both eyes were open.

"Yeah, you know... Besides the therapist. Just someone random. Like you used to."

He sat up, his body tense. "I don't know, Ains."

"What do you mean, you don't know?"

"I'm just not really feeling it right now."

"Why not?"

He pushed up from the bed, unbuttoning his shirt with his back to me.

"I just told you I'm exhausted. Work's been hectic. It's just not a good time."

"So let me help take your mind off of things." I tried to ease him out of his shirt.

"I said no, okay?" His tone was sharper than I'd ever heard it, cracking through the air.

I took a step back as if I'd been slapped. "Have... Have I done something wrong?" I felt vulnerable, an emotion that made me sick. I'd never been one to beg for anyone's attention, but I'd done it with Peter for the sake of our kids. For the sake of our marriage.

The desire to keep it up was waning fast.

"No, you haven't done anything wrong." His eyes were apologetic as he moved forward, kissing my cheek. "I'm sorry I snapped. I just don't want to do it right now, okay? You'll be the first to know when I do."

"Well, what if I want to?"

Did I?

Did it matter?

He shook his head. "Stop it. Okay? Just stop. We have to be smart about this. Let's just let it all die down for a bit, and then maybe in a few months..."

"Maybe in a few months, what? You'll be able to look at me again? To touch me? To fuck me?"

"Keep your voice down." He groaned, wincing. He may as well have gagged.

"Peter, please, can you just look at me?" I begged. I

hated this version of myself. I hated who he was turning me into.

He turned to look at me finally, his eyes practically glazing over. "What do you want from me, Ainsley? *What?*"

I opened my mouth, prepared to say so much, but I didn't know where to start. "Is it because of Joanna? Because I said no? Because if that's what it'll take to fix whatever's wrong, let's just do it. Whatever you want." I didn't know if I meant it, but I needed to see what he'd say. It seemed as if everything had changed from the moment we met her.

"It's not about her." His face drew down into a scowl. "God, I haven't thought about her since our session. Work has just been crazy. I just need a minute, okay? Nothing's wrong with us. I swear." He lowered his voice, stepping forward and taking my hands. He kissed my cheek, my hands, my fingers. "I love you. We're fine. Everything's fine. Don't worry so much, okay?" He squeezed my hands, then dropped them and turned away, pulling off his shirt without another word.

Conversation over.

Except it was far from over.

And we were far from fine.

CHAPTER TWENTY-SIX

PETER

"You seem different this evening. Is everything okay?" Joanna asked, watching me from across the room. I'd spent most of the session pacing after my fight with Ainsley, but I didn't want to tell her that.

I didn't want to talk about Ainsley at all, truth be told.

"Yeah, everything's fine." I took a seat, trying to quiet my fidgeting. "Just a rough week at work."

"Want to talk about it?"

"I don't want to bore you."

Her smile was stiff. She seemed tired.

"How are things at home? Have you thought about bringing Annie back for a session?"

"You know I can't do that," I said with a scoff.

"She won't come?"

Why was she talking about Ainsley so much? Why did she care? Wasn't I enough for her?

"Truth be told, I don't know how much longer we're going to be together."

She sucked in a gasp, obviously concerned. Or was she excited? I couldn't tell. We both knew she wanted me.

In due time, Joanna.

"I'm sorry to hear that."

"Don't be sorry."

She cocked her head to the side, teasing me. "Why's that?"

"You know why…" I growled, standing up and moving toward her. I sat on the table between us. For a moment, I thought she might scold me, but instead, she sat still. A smile formed on her lips.

"She doesn't understand you…" she said.

You understand me. Don't you, Joanna?

"She doesn't," I admitted, swallowing. "Not like you."

The smile faded from her lips momentarily, her doe eyes staring up at me from behind thick, dark lashes— wanting me, teasing me. She was daring me to go for it. To cross the line we never had.

I leaned forward, ever so slowly.

"Not like me," she confirmed.

"We shouldn't…" I told her, leaning forward more. We shouldn't, but we didn't care. She closed her eyes, giving me all the permission I needed. In seconds, my mouth was on hers. I cupped her face with both hands, parting her lips with my tongue. Her breaths were shaky with passion and anticipation.

I released her, sitting back on the table.

"Why'd you stop?" she asked, her lips red.

If I didn't, I might never be able to.

"We have to take this slow," I warned, though slow was the last speed I wanted to take. I wanted her then and now, but if there was one thing I knew, it was that nothing was ever as exciting as the first time with someone new.

Joanna deserved the perfect first time.

She pushed out her bottom lip, pouting, and I popped it with my finger. "Nice girls don't beg."

She batted her eyelashes at me playfully. "Who says I'm a nice girl?"

I pressed my lips to hers one last time, then forced myself to step away. "You are a nice girl, Joanna. That's why I want to do this right. I can't...I can't stop thinking about you."

"I feel the same way."

"I know we didn't meet in the most ideal way, but however we came together, I'm just so glad we did."

"So, tell Annie the truth."

"You don't understand."

"Understand what?" she asked, shaking her head.

"She'd never let me go. Not ever."

"Don't be ridiculous. It's obvious you're not happy. People get divorced all the time."

"Not Annie."

"What do you mean? What could she possibly do?"

I began pacing, trying to think. "She'd do anything to keep me. She's dangerous. If she knew about you, about us, she'd kill you."

Fear flickered in her eyes, and I returned to her. "Don't worry. That's why we're taking this slow. It's to protect you."

"You wouldn't let her hurt me, would you?" she asked, not appearing entirely reassured.

I sat down in front of her again, my hands on her knees. "I'll always protect you, Joanna. But you have to trust me on this. You have to let me handle her."

"I do trust you," she vowed. "Of course I do."

"Good."

"And you can trust me."

I nodded. I knew I could. "I do trust you."

"Then that's all that matters. We'll be together when we can."

I smiled at her. "As soon as we can."

CHAPTER TWENTY-SEVEN

AINSLEY

"Hey, love, what are you up to?"

It had been weeks since I'd heard from Glennon, and it felt so good to hear her voice. I leaned forward, turning up the car's speaker.

"I've just left work and am on my way to therapy. What about you? Where are you jet setting this week?"

She laughed. "Oh, I don't know. I can't keep track anymore. I swear, it's no wonder Seth has always been so exhausted. I don't even remember if I ate breakfast today."

"You'd be *hangry* if you didn't," I teased. "Maybe you should ask Seth."

"Ha." She gave a sarcastic laugh. "I miss you."

"I miss you, too. When are you coming home? I want to do a whole big thing."

"Oh, you don't have to do a big thing. A quiet night with pizza and beer sounds amazing to me."

I mock gasped. "What? Hate to break it to you, sister, but pizza isn't typically vegan."

"Eh, well, that lasted all of a month."

"Seriously, when are you coming home?"

"We're going to try and squeeze in a weekend next month."

"Next month? Really? That's so far away..." I had so much I wanted to talk to her about, but I couldn't do it over the phone.

"Well, we were supposed to come down this weekend, but um"—she cleared her throat—"Seth actually introduced me to one of his coworkers in Canada, and he's taking me out for dinner this weekend."

She said it casually, as if it were no big deal.

"What? You met someone? And he lives in *Canada?"*

"I know. Am I crazy? Is it crazy? Seth thought it was a good idea. He's this really nice guy. An investment banker. Single dad. Has the whole two-point-five kids and a dog. Picket fence. Yada yada."

I winced. "Kids and a dog? Is he divorced?"

"Widowed."

We released sympathetic sighs at the same time. "Poor guy."

"Tell me about it," she agreed.

"As much as I hate it, he sounds pretty perfect for you."

"Yeah?"

"Yeah. Of course. You've always wanted kids. And a dog. And, hell, Canada's got free healthcare. Maybe I'll move up there with you."

"Well, no one's moving yet, but we'll be sure to build you a guesthouse."

"Let him know you're a package deal."

She laughed. "Will do. Seriously, though, I miss you guys so much."

I put the car in park. "We miss you too, G. We'll see you soon, okay?"

"It's a date."

"Okay, well, I hate to let you go, but I just got to therapy and I don't want to be late."

She let out a playful groan. "Okay. Fine. Go get mentally healthy."

I snorted. "Love you."

"Love you more."

With that, I ended the call and stepped out of the car. Once inside, I greeted her first, though she had her back to me.

"Hey, Joanna."

"Hey, Annie," she said gently, her voice hoarse as she glanced over her shoulder, seeming startled to see me. Had she been sleeping recently? Or crying?

"Everything okay?"

She cleared her throat as I took a seat. "Yep. Sorry. How are you? How was your day?"

"Well, I just found out my best friend is probably going to move to Canada and become best friends with a moose or something, so there's that."

She furrowed her brow. "What?"

I waved it off. "Nothing. I'm joking."

"Your best friend... That's the one you mentioned before? The one you spend most of your time with?"

I nodded, tears stinging my eyes at the thought of her. "At least, I used to."

"What happened?"

"There was this whole thing with her husband, er, ex-husband. They had a rough patch, then a divorce. Now they're closer than ever and traveling the world together."

"That seems…healthy."

"Surprisingly, they're probably the healthiest couple I know."

"Are you including yourself in that?"

I glanced at her, then looked away, refusing to answer.

After a moment, she went on. "You must miss her."

"Every day." My voice broke as I said it, and I swiped my cheek against my shoulder.

"When did you see her last?"

"It's been like seven or eight months, I guess." I tried to do the mental math.

"Was she the person you used to talk to when you and Pete had problems?"

I nodded.

"Who do you talk to now?"

"You?" It was a question, rather than a definitive answer.

She pursed her lips. "Maybe you should go see her. Tell her what's going on."

"I can't do that."

"Why not?"

"Because!" I exploded. Why was she forcing the issue? "Because she deserves to be happy for once without my problems interfering."

"I'm sure she doesn't think you're interfering."

"Of course she doesn't. Because that's not who she is. But I can't do that to her. I made this mess. It's my fault. I have to fix it now."

"And how are you going to do that?"

"I haven't decided." I took a sip of the tea I'd brought with me.

"Have you tried to talk to Pete? To tell him you're unhappy?"

"You don't understand…"

"I'm trying to."

"He's not the kind of person you can just leave. The things we've done to each other, with each other—"

"The *fencing*?" she asked, a lilt in her voice that told me she knew we weren't actually talking about fencing when we'd brought it up.

"Among other things…"

"You just need to talk to each other. Maybe the two of you want the same things without realizing it. Maybe you're so busy protecting each other that you can't see the truth right in front of you."

"And what truth would that be?"

She hesitated. The room was eerily quiet, just the ticking clock on the wall to keep us company. "Do you love him, Annie? Are you in love with your husband?"

I locked my jaw, refusing to think about the question.

It was too painful.

It hurt too badly to admit the truth, even to myself.

"Have you asked him if he loves you?"

I jerked back as if I'd been slapped. "Excuse me?"

"I'm just trying to point out that—"

"You don't have any idea what you're talking about," I said. "You don't know anything about my marriage."

"Of course not. I'm just saying—"

"Well, don't." I stood, storming past her. "Don't *just say*."

"Where are you going?"

"Home. Goodbye, Joanna."

"Wait—" she called after me, but it was too late. I was done.

Done with her.

Done with everything.

I'D ONLY BEEN in the kitchen a few minutes, still dressed in my work clothes, when I heard a knock on the door. I'd left work early for therapy, so it was not yet time for Peter or the kids to be home.

Who could be at the door, then?

I dried my hands on the towel near the stove, then crossed the room, jogging toward the front door. I pulled back the curtain, my body going cold at the sight of a woman in a dark suit standing just beyond the glass, looking very official.

The woman waved at me when she noticed my movement. I closed the curtain and, seeing no alternative, opened the door just a hair.

"Can I help you?" I asked, now filled with a new kind of worry.

"Are you Mrs. Greenburg? Ainsley Greenburg?"

"Yes, that's me."

"I'm Detective LaToya Burks," she said, handing over a business card. "Is your husband home?" She peered past me into the house.

"He's at work. Is something wrong? Is it the kids?"

Her eyes darted back to meet mine. "No, ma'am.

They're fine. I'm actually here about a man named Chris Henson. Do you know him?"

My heart sank. I blinked. Breathed in slowly. "Chris Henson..." I let the name linger on my tongue. "You don't mean Coach Chris, do you? Our daughter's dance coach?"

"That's the one." She pointed at me.

"Um, well, yes. Of course I know him. He's been coaching my daughter all of her life. Except this year, she'd kind of gotten bored with it. But we love Coach Chris. Why? Is he okay? Did something happen?"

"Do you mind if I come inside?" She pointed behind me, and I stepped back instantly, allowing her past me.

"No, not at all. I'm sorry. I'm a bit frazzled. Come in." I gestured toward the couch. "Please, sit. Can I get you something to drink?"

"I'm fine," she assured me. "If you want to sit as well. I just have a few questions to go over."

"That sounds...serious."

She clicked her pen, pulling out a notepad. "When was the last time you saw Chris Henson?"

"Um, I don't know... It's been a while. Over a year, probably. As I said, my daughter dropped dance class and that was really the only time we saw him."

She pursed her lips as she wrote. "Do you ever recall seeing Chris getting into heated arguments with the parents? Were there any incidents or parents that stand out to you as particularly disagreeable?"

"No," I said quickly. "Everyone loves him. He's always been great with the girls. Lots of private sessions... He'd take them out for ice cream after practice."

Something lit up in the detective's eyes, and I knew I

was onto something. She pursed her lips, scrawling a note onto the paper in her hands.

"And did your daughter ever mention anything to you about him behaving inappropriately? Maybe something he said or did? Did he ever text your daughter about practice or...anything like that?"

My eyes widened with apparent shock. "No, never. She was sad to stop going, honestly. And she's only eleven, so she's just recently gotten a cell phone. She only texts her friends. Why do you ask?"

She jotted down something else, ignoring the question.

"Can you tell me what's going on? Please? Sh-should I be worried?"

"Right now, I can't say much. But if you do hear from the coach—"

"Wait, if I hear from him? Can you not find him? Maisy mentioned that he'd left, but I just thought she meant vacation."

"I'm afraid right now we haven't been able to locate him or his girlfriend."

"Girlfriend?"

"Joanna St. James. Do you know her?"

"The name doesn't sound familiar..." I pretended to search my memory.

"Okay, that's okay. It's Chris we really need to find. Apparently, no one has seen Chris in about a month, but Joanna was last seen by family and friends two weeks ago."

"Oh no. Do you think they could be in danger?"

Her jaw tightened. "Right now it's an open investigation, so we're exploring all our options. The most important thing is that we're able to get in touch with Chris as soon as possible regarding a few allegations."

"Allegations? What do you mean? Is he in trouble?"

She gave me a patronizing grin. "Again, I'm not at liberty to say, but if you do hear from him, could you call me right away? You have my number." She pointed toward the business card still in my hand.

"Yes. Of course." I stared at it.

"And if your daughter mentions anything…"

"Yes, we'll call you right away. Do you need to speak with her?" I winced internally as I offered.

Please say no.

Please say no.

"That won't be necessary. I think I've taken up enough of your time." She placed the notepad and pen in her jacket pocket and stood. "Thank you for talking with me."

"Of course. And if there's anything I could do, just let me know. I'm the manager of a bank downtown, so I know quite a few people around here. I could ask around, see if anyone's heard from him."

If it was possible, her expression softened even more. I was a bank manager, not a killer. It was obvious I couldn't pose a threat to anyone.

"Don't go to any trouble. Just keep an eye out for him. And talk to your daughter about Internet safety… Lots of freaks out there. You can never be too careful."

"Thank you, Detective." I shut the door behind her, watching through the glass as she made her way out to the unmarked car. My heart raced as I waited for her to leave, my breathing erratic and petrified. As the car finally pulled down the driveway and out of sight, I felt my pulse slow.

It was okay.

It was all okay.

At least that meant they were looking for him because someone had turned him in, not because they thought he'd been murdered.

Once again, it seemed we were going to get away with everything.

I turned back toward the kitchen, searching for something to make for dinner while I prepared myself for how I would bring this up to Peter.

It was amazing just how much you could hide behind the mask of a normal, boring life.

CHAPTER TWENTY-EIGHT

PETER

S he looked tired tonight.

She hadn't been sleeping well, I knew.

"Hello, beautiful," I said, kissing the top of her head. She glanced up at me, her dark hair falling into her eyes.

"Hey, handsome," she said, her voice hoarse.

"You sound sleepy."

"I wish you'd bring me to bed with you," she cooed.

"I wish I could do that."

She smiled, wiggling her shoulders playfully. As best she could, anyway. "You could, you know. You could take me inside right now. Have your way with me." She winked.

"Don't tempt me."

"Come here." She lifted her chin, beckoning me to her.

I stood, crossing the room and touching her chin. She no longer smelled like soap, but only of me. She was dressed in my clothes, her lips had been claimed by me. Her body. Her thoughts.

I was all she wanted.

All she could think of.

I pressed our mouths together, biting her lower lip until she cried out. The metallic tinge of blood rested on my tongue.

"Take me inside, Peter. Let's go. Let's be together."

"You know I can't, Joanna," I told her, slipping the sleeve of my shirt from her shoulder. She had purple and green bruises from my last visit, and I placed my mouth in a clear space, biting down once more. When I was finished with her, her body would be a canvas of purples, greens, and yellows.

My little masterpiece.

"When will you let me out?" she whimpered.

Once so full of life, she'd become a shell of herself. It always happened that way. This was how it always went.

This room changed them.

These walls.

They'd fight in the beginning, or in Joanna's case, they'd try to play along, try to outsmart me, to pretend to want to be with me. From the moment I'd brought her here, the day she'd figured out *fencing* wasn't fencing, she'd begun to change. She'd been everything I wanted in the beginning, saying everything I wanted to hear, but in the end, just like all the others, this was what I was left with.

A sniveling, whining, shadow of the woman I'd chosen in the first place.

The woman I'd deemed special.

"You're safe in here," I told her, gesturing around the secret room. "Safe from her."

"She won't hurt me. You'll protect me. We can take care of her."

She didn't know my wife at all, but it was fun to amuse her. I stood, running my thumb across her cheekbone. It stuck out more now than it once had. "We will someday. I've told you, we have to be smart. You want to be with me, don't you?"

"More than anything," she swore, brushing her cheek across my stomach. "That's all I want."

She was teasing me, but it wouldn't work. In this room, I had all the self-restraint in the world.

I was a god here.

The whole world.

I had all the time I needed.

She was at my beck and call.

Whenever I finally took her, it would be everything I wanted it to be.

For that, we still had to wait.

Just a bit longer. The waiting was the fun part here.

Time stood still.

I drug out our time together because I knew, soon enough, it would be over.

Soon enough, I'd go back to my regular life and Joanna… Joanna would have to go to the woods.

CHAPTER TWENTY-NINE

AINSLEY

"You seem distracted tonight," I whispered, handing Peter a glass of wine as I sat down next to him on the sofa.

"Do I?" He took a sip, eyes locked on the TV.

"Yeah…"

He didn't respond, but leaned his head over toward my shoulder as if to placate me. Was it all just a habit with him? Was he only doing what he thought I wanted him to?

Where did he go when his mind wandered?

How often had I accepted him physically when mentally he refused to stay with me?

"Hey, did I tell you I heard from Glennon?"

"You did?"

"Mhm. Apparently she met someone in Canada."

"Canada?" He wrinkled his nose. "What's she going to do with someone up there?"

"I have no idea. They're just going to dinner."

I'd killed for the man I loved, and he was acting like it was ridiculous to get on a flight for someone.

"Hm."

"I, um, I didn't want to bring it up in front of the kids, but," I lowered my voice, "a detective came by earlier today."

He tensed, turning his head to look at me and muting the TV. I lifted up, so we were eye to eye. "A detective?"

"Yeah, asking about Coach Chris."

"And you didn't think to mention that until now?" He set his glass of wine down on the coffee table, sloshing a bit of it out onto the wood.

"It wasn't a big deal. She asked if Maisy had ever mentioned anything about him being inappropriate."

"What did you say?"

"I said no, of course."

"And what else?" A wrinkle had formed on his forehead.

"That was basically it. She gave me her card and asked us to call if we heard anything from him. She said that no one's heard from him in a while and they want to ask him some questions."

"Did she seem suspicious of you?"

"No," I said quickly. "Not at all. I told her we loved Coach and he'd been good to Maisy. I might've dropped a few mentions of him doing a lot of private sessions to really lay it on, but—"

"You what?" His hand went into the air in disbelief. "You shouldn't have done that."

"Oh, it was fine."

"You don't know that. What if she thinks you know something now?"

"She doesn't, Peter. Jesus, calm down."

He picked his glass back up, moving farther from me on the couch. For once, I didn't follow him.

"Oh, there was one more thing. She, um, she did mention that his girlfriend is missing as well. Joanna." I cocked my head to the side. "Had you heard anything about that?"

"No." He scowled. "Why would I?"

"I don't know, I just thought you might've..."

"Well, I haven't. Don't know why I would've."

I stared at him, taking in the profile of his face, the curve of his lips. Lips I'd once loved to kiss. His hand gripped the wineglass the way it had once held me.

Who were we kidding anymore?

Why was I still holding on to an illusion that there was something I could do to make him change? To make him love me again?

Once, I'd thought a loyalty to me would be enough, thought staying together no matter what would be enough.

Now, I knew differently. For so long, I'd thought I could love him hard enough to fix him. All the while, he was breaking me.

I stood up, kissing his temple.

"Where are you going?" he asked.

"To get a refill." I wiggled my glass at him as I crossed the room. In the kitchen, I began to pour myself another glass of wine.

"Bring me some, will you?"

I stopped, staring at the wine bottle and remembering

the many nights we'd shared glasses of wine to celebrate special occasions. I thought back over the many bottles we'd been gifted at our wedding, the times he'd order my favorite wine at a restaurant before I'd had the chance, the birthdays and anniversaries where we'd opened a bottle once the house had gone quiet and the kids were down for bed.

Things had been good once, they truly had.

I wasn't delusional.

I could remember him. Before.

Before it all changed.

When I was the whole world to him.

But we hadn't been those people in a long time. It was time to stop kidding myself.

WHEN I MADE it back into the living room with just the bottle in my hand, it took a second for him to notice me.

"Where's your glass?"

"I think I'm just going to go to bed."

"Why? What's wrong?"

"I have a headache."

"Hm… Want me to get you some medicine?"

"Nah, I think it's from the wine. Lying down will help." I paused—one last-ditch effort on my tongue. "Want to join me?"

"I want to catch the news," he said simply. "I'll be in there soon, though."

I nodded, placing the wine bottle down in front of him. No sooner had I done so than he'd scooped it up and filled his glass to the brim. I kissed his head one last time.

"I love you."

"Love you, too." He barely glanced my way, breaking my heart for the final time as I headed for the bedroom.

Once I had, I grabbed a bag and began to pack.

CHAPTER THIRTY

PETER

Darkness.
The world was dark.
Damp.

Cold.

Rank.

Something smelled.

My eyes were so dry, it was painful to open them. When I finally did, I opened one eye first, the heaviness in my head unlike anything I'd ever experienced before. Trying to blink only caused me more pain. I wanted to rub my eyes, but I was lying on my hand.

No, wait.

I wasn't lying on anything.

I was sitting up.

And my hands were stuck behind me.

Both of my eyes were open then, trying to make sense of what I was seeing.

"Joanna?"

Her dark hair cascaded over her face in front of me.

"Joanna?" I groaned, trying to pull myself from sleep.

Why was I so tired?

Why was I in this room?

The room.

My room.

What the hell was happening with my hands?

I struggled to pull them free, but found I had no strength.

Why wasn't she answering me?

"That sedative's pretty strong, hm?" The voice came from behind me, and I jolted awake.

"Ainsley?" I tried to look behind me, but I couldn't see a thing. The room was cloaked in darkness.

Shadows.

"What the hell is going on?" I demanded.

"Shouldn't waste your strength," she said, clicking her tongue.

"Is this a joke?" I remembered what she'd said. "You sedated me?"

"Just a drop in your wine. You're not the only one who hung on to some of the sedatives after we killed Chris. I warned you about what would happen if you ever lied to me again."

As she said it, I remembered Joanna. I glanced at her, still sitting in the chair I'd tied her to. Ainsley must've known I'd sedated her to get her there, but how did she know she was there in the first place?

"What are you talking about?"

"Did you honestly think I didn't know you were still seeing Joanna?" Her voice was getting closer now. "I know the signs, Peter. I know how you get when you've got

211

someone new to obsess over. The way you withdraw. The way you begin to ignore me. Ignore the kids." She scoffed. "I guess we both had the same idea, going to see her separately. Problem was, I wanted to see her to help us. You only wanted to see her to help yourself."

"That's not true—"

"So, when I went to one of our sessions and Taylor said she'd gone on personal leave and hadn't told her when she'd be back, I just knew I'd find her here." I watched her move beside me, her shoes sliding on the concrete. Finally, she was in view, a knife in her hand. "I hoped I would be wrong, but I wasn't. So, I continued my sessions here, same as you. By then, though, I was starting to realize I didn't know what it was I was fighting for anymore." She twisted her wrist, swinging the knife this way and that.

I swallowed, keeping my eyes trained on it. "What are you doing with that?"

"I was never going to be enough for you, was I?" She shook her head, looking bemused. "No matter what I did. No matter what I promised. No matter how understanding I was... This was never about me." She twirled the end of the knife on her finger.

"Just put that down, so we can talk."

"I thought if I proved to you that I was with you—no matter what—I just knew that finally you'd let me in. That things would go back to normal. But you don't *do* normal, do you, Peter? Normal isn't exciting enough for you? See, you can tell me all these lies about how it isn't about attraction, it's all about power, but..." She huffed. "I gave you the power. I backed off. I did everything right. I let you control it."

"Control what?"

"Everything!" she shouted, swatting her leg. "Our lives. Us. Everything. I played the doting little wife, and it still wasn't enough." She let out an exasperated sigh. "And that's when I realized this was never about me. It was always...about...you." She pointed the tip of the knife at me. "See, I thought I could fix you. I thought somehow you were different from Chris and Jim and all these other monsters, because you had a good side. A loving side." She faked a pout. "But I'm realizing that those sides don't matter."

"Of course they do—"

"They don't." She shook her head, backing away from me. "I will always love you, Peter, because you gave me our kids. And you gave them the best of yourself. But there is something deeply wrong with you. Something no amount of whatever I can do will fix. Turns out I'm not as good a fixer as I thought."

"What are you saying?"

"I'm saying I'm done. I'm done trying. I'm done stressing. I'm taking my kids and doing what I should've done all those years ago when I found out what you were doing." She bent over her knees, her hair dangling toward the floor as she released an exhausted gasp. "I can't believe it's taken me this long to do it."

"Ains, I'm not like them... Look, you're not making sense. I know you're mad. I should've told you about Joanna, but she means nothing to me. I just wanted to protect you from her. I didn't want you to have to be involved in any more—"

"Shut up!" she bellowed, moving toward me with the knife again. "Enough of your lies and your *protection*, Peter. The only thing I ever needed to be protected from was you."

"That's not true, that's not—"

"It is. It *is* true."

She wasn't making any sense. She wasn't being rational. I just needed her to calm down. To listen to me. I could make her understand. If she knew that Joanna had figured out the truth—that we'd never actually meant *fencing*—she'd understand. She had to.

"I never touched Joanna. Do you hear me? I had her here, not because I was obsessed with her, but because I wanted to keep her away from the police. I did that for you! For Maisy! You can ask her yourself. She'll tell you—"

"No, I don't think I can." She cut me off, giving a wide shake of her head with a maniacal grin on her lips.

"What are you talking about?" My chest felt hollow.

"I'm sorry, Peter. If there was any other way, believe me, I'd have found it by now. But I can't do this. I can't keep living like this."

"Living like what? What are you talking about? What are you going to do?" I scoffed. "Kill me? C'mon, Ains, we love each other. We're in this together, right? A team? This is just a misunderstanding."

"You're right about one thing, Peter. There has been a misunderstanding... For several years now. But at this exact moment, I'm clearer than I've ever been. I don't want to be on a team with you. And you don't really want to be on a team with me, either. For so long, I've wished you would. For so long. But wishing isn't doing me any good anymore. You've shown me who you are, and now, I have to make a choice about who *I* am." She jabbed her finger into her chest.

"Please, let's just talk. What's your plan? You have to at least have a plan… Let's just figure this out. We can always figure things out, right? Ains? You and me?"

"I don't need your help. I have a plan. I'm going to take the kids on a long vacation. When we come back, the house will have burned to the ground."

Fear gripped my organs. Was she insane?

I took solace in the fact that if she burned the house, this room wouldn't burn with it. It was concrete on every side. We'd be safe. But would I starve? I tried to calculate in my head how long I could last. How long would it take me to free myself?

As if she'd read my mind, she added, "I'll start two fires. One in here, one in the house… You'll have been supposed to join us, but we'll return home when we start to worry. I've already typed out your goodbye email—well, more of a confession really—and scheduled it to send after we leave. The guilt of it all was just too much for you to bear." She was emotionless as she said it. Cold and calculating.

"It's the middle of the night. You can't take them on vacation now. They'll know something's up. You aren't being rational."

"Oh, don't worry. We aren't leaving now. I'm going to tell them you got sent away for work and we'll leave in a few days to meet you. But then, you'll get sent away again before we get there." She waved a hand as if to say it was too much to explain. "It's a whole thing. But that's the beauty of this room, isn't it? No one will know you're here. You can scream and shout and beg and cry... And no one will *ever* know." She gave an accepting nod. "Well, no one but me, obviously. It's kind of full circle, really. I'm sure you can't appreciate the humor right now, but, you know...maybe someday." She winced. "Or not."

"You can't do this. You're not this person."

"Correction: I *wasn't* this person. But you made me into her." She rested her hands on her hips, staring into space as the realization hit her. "It *really* is full circle, isn't it? I'm killing you because you taught me how. And I'm doing it in the room where you killed a whole lotta people." She chuckled, flipping her hair over her shoulder and glancing at the clock. "Anyway, we should probably get this over with." She reached into her pocket and pulled out another syringe. "You shouldn't feel a thing. I promise, I'm going to make it peaceful. I'll at least give you that courtesy."

"Ainsley, wait! Please." She moved toward me, and I caught the glint of tears in her eyes. I could stop her. I could reason with her. She was close to breaking. I could break her. "Please. I love you. I love you. I swear. Think about the kids. Think about Maisy. They need me. They need their dad. Who's going to walk her down the aisle? You can't do this. Come on... What about our future? Our grandkids? Their graduations. Please. Please. You don't want to do this. Trust me, you can't handle it. It'll destroy you! Please. I love you! God, I love you so much! Please don't do this!"

She grabbed hold of my neck. "You've given me no choice."

"I love you. Please, baby, please..." She lowered the syringe into my neck as I fought back, jerking and pulling at the ropes that bound my hands.

"You don't have to do this," I pleaded. "I'll give you a divorce if that's what you want. I'll go away and you'll never hear from me again. Just say the word and I'm gone. You can have everything—the house, the kids, whatever you—"

"Better a widow, with two and a half kids and a dog, than divorced." She smiled at a joke I didn't quite understand.

The room had begun to spin, my head feeling heavy. The injection site stung as she drew the needle out of my skin. "You...called...me the monster, but...you're a monster...too."

My vision grew fuzzy as I felt her lips on mine for what I knew would be the last time. Cool tears dripped from her cheeks to mine. She patted my face, sniffling.

"Maybe I am. Maybe we both are. But you, Peter, you created this monster. And now I have to be brave enough to kill it." She released my cheek, letting my face fall forward.

Try as I might, I couldn't summon the strength to lift it back up.

It was then I recognized the smell in the room.

The blood.

I scanned the portion of the room I could see and saw the pool of crimson under Joanna's chair.

She was already gone.

I'd been robbed of the chance to end her life. Maybe that stung worst of all.

I closed my eyes, beginning to feel weak. Was I going to die from the sedative, starvation, or the fire? She hadn't been clear.

I smiled to myself despite the fear. I had to hand it to her. If there was a way to go, I guessed this was it.

At the hands of the woman I'd made a wife, mother, and killer.

Full circle.

CHAPTER THIRTY-ONE

AINSLEY

SIX DAYS LATER

"You need sunscreen," I shouted across the beach at the boys as they ignored me, continuing to splash in the ocean water without a care in the world.

Maisy looked over at me from where she lay on a towel, book in her hand. "Ooh, Mom, look! The chocolate-covered banana stand just opened. Want to get one?" She pointed down the beach with glee, and I shielded my eyes from the sun, trying to see what she was talking about.

Spying it, I grinned at her. Normally, I might've said no. That she might spoil her dinner. Or I might've turned one down for myself. Now though, nothing could bring me down.

"Race ya," I teased, sticking out my tongue as I scrambled to my feet. We darted across the blazing hot sand as fast as our legs would carry us. When we reached the stand, both panting and exhausted, we were laughing too hard to catch our breath enough to order.

I held up two fingers to the teen behind the counter and passed over a ten-dollar bill.

"You win," I said, when I'd finally caught my breath, though it had been close to a tie.

"Legs of a dancer," she teased.

He handed us our snacks and we made our way back to the spot we'd claimed earlier that day.

As we walked, Maisy grinned at me.

I bumped her hip with mine. "You look happy."

"I am," she confirmed.

"Yeah?"

"Yeah. I'm so glad we came. I've missed this place."

"Me too." I licked a bit of chocolate from my fingertip. "We're going to have to start coming back more often."

"You mean it?" Her eyes lit up, sending a wave of joy crashing into my chest.

"Mhm. If you guys want to."

"Always."

"It's a deal, then. Family trips to the beach way more often." We flopped down onto the towels.

"Speaking of, when is Dad supposed to be coming?"

My joy evaporated. I hadn't gotten over the sting of guilt every time they asked about him, but I had my answers and expressions prepared. I smiled. "He'll be here tomorrow or the next day. Just as soon as he can get away from his new project. But hey, we're having fun here, just the four of us, aren't we?"

She nodded, picking up her book again. "Yeah. Maybe we should just move here."

I let the thought wash over me. "You know, maybe we will."

She stared at me as if I'd spoken a new language. "Seriously?"

"Would you like that?"

"Uh, yeah!"

"Alright, I'll talk to your dad."

Her jaw hung open. "Are you joking? Just like that?"

"Sure," I said. "No promises, but I think it's time for a new chapter, don't you?"

"What's changed about you?" she asked, narrowing her eyes at me.

"What do you mean?"

"You're so different lately."

"Good different, I hope?"

"Very good." She eyed her book, the latest in a long line of horror stories I'd picked up for her at the book-store yesterday. "Unless you've been replaced by a cyborg."

"Worse. An alien, and I've come to bring you back to my home planet." I lunged for her, tickling her as she rolled away from me, falling into a fit of giggles.

"Mom, stop!" she cried, laughing so hard it brought tears to her eyes. There was sand all over our food when we were done, but I didn't care. Nothing could ruin my mood.

Nothing could take the sunshine out of the trip.

Noticing the fun we were having, the boys jogged up the beach and toward us.

"Oh, nice!" Dylan said, spying our food. "I want one."

Riley licked his lips. "Me too."

"Get two more for us, would you?" I pulled cash from my pocket. "These are ruined."

"Come with me?" Dylan asked, and Riley tagged along happily.

Things were really good now.

I didn't know why I hadn't seen that possibility before.

I'd made horrible choices, ones I'd have to live with forever.

But as long as I had my kids, I could live with whatever came my way. Of that, more than anything else, I was sure.

In my pocket, my phone buzzed.

I pulled it out, staring at a text message on the screen. A lump formed in my chest.

No.

"Who is it?" Maisy asked, spying my hesitation.

I flashed her a smile and opened the text, staring at a picture I couldn't quite make out. I zoomed in closer.

It was a blueprint, from what I could tell, but I was only looking at a small section of it. Something that had been circled.

Underneath it, a scrawled note made the hairs on my arms stand on end.

"What is it?" Maisy asked again, more forcefully this time. "You okay?"

I was no longer listening to her, instead focusing all my energy on the message written in handwriting I would've recognized anywhere.

Finally, I understood what I was staring at. He'd circled a space along the wall in the hidden room that read *Emergency Exit (Hidden)*.

I stopped breathing, a chill sweeping through me. I read over his message twice.

No.

No.

No.

No.

NoNoNoNoNoNoNo.

It wasn't possible. It wasn't.

And yet it was real.

His message was simple, yet abundantly clear.

I'd lost.

The plan had failed.

I read it once more, feeling as if I were going to be sick.

Sorry, honey.
We're in this together, remember?
After all, rules are rules.
Guess I had just one more secret.
How's that for full circle?

THERE'S MORE TO THE STORY...

It was the perfect marriage...
until it all fell apart.

We're not done yet...
Read the complete #1 bestselling ARRANGEMENT
trilogy today:
mybook.to/arrangementnovels

DON'T MISS THE NEXT
PSYCHOLOGICAL THRILLER FROM
KIERSTEN MODGLIN!

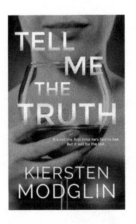

It's not the first time he's lied to her.
But it will be the last.

Order *Tell Me the Truth* today:
mybook.to/tmtt

ENJOYED THE AMENDMENT?

If you enjoyed this story, please consider leaving me a quick review. It doesn't have to be long—just a few words will do. Who knows? Your review might be the thing that encourages a future reader to take a chance on my work!
To leave a review, please visit:
http://mybook.to/theamendment

Let everyone know how much you loved
The Amendment on Goodreads:
https://bit.ly/3mJJm9b

DON'T MISS THE NEXT RELEASE FROM KIERSTEN MODGLIN

Thank you so much for reading this story. I'd love to invite you to sign up for my mailing list and text alerts so we can be sure you don't miss my next release.

Sign up for my mailing list here:
http://eepurl.com/dhiRRv

Sign up for my text alerts here:
www.kierstenmodglinauthor.com/textalerts.html

ACKNOWLEDGMENTS

Ainsley and Peter's story wouldn't exist without the love, support, and encouragement of so many people—

First and foremost, I'd like to thank my incredible husband and wonderful little girl—thank you for being you. For giving me inspiration, laughs, and reasons to come out of the writing cave. I love you both so incredibly much and I'm the luckiest woman in the world to be able to do this life with the two of you.

To my friend, Emerald O'Brien—thank you for being my best friend and loudest cheerleader. Thank you for celebrating every idea, for never getting tired of my indecision and inability to take a break, for the hours-long conversations and late night Skype calls. Thank you for always, always believing I can do anything, even when I struggle to believe it myself. I love you, friend.

To my immensely talented editor, Sarah West—thank you for shining up every story, for understanding my vision, and always trusting my instincts. I'm grateful for your insights, advice, and belief in me.

To the proofreading team at My Brother's Editor— thank you for being the final set of eyes on my stories and always helping them to shine that much brighter.

To my loyal readers (AKA the #KMod Squad)—I still can't believe how lucky I am to have our community.

You're everything I dreamed of having in readers and so much more. Your loyalty to me and my wild stories is unfathomable. I'm so blessed and so incredibly grateful to have readers like you. Thank you for coming back story after story, for trusting me to take you down a dark and slippery slope and always reveal a satisfying, unpredictable truth eventually. Thank you for making my books bestsellers and for shouting about them from the rooftops to everyone who will listen. I love you all.

To Carly, Olivia, Layne, and Kate—thank you for loving The Arrangement so much. Thank you for believing in the story I wanted to tell and for giving me the encouragement I needed to write Book 2.

To LaToya Burks—a sweet reader who let me borrow her name for this dark and twisted thriller. Thank you for trusting me with it. I had a blast adding LaToya into this story and I hope you enjoyed seeing your namesake brought to life.

Last but certainly not least, to you—thank you for purchasing this book and supporting my art. Thank you for taking a chance on this wild, scandalous world. Whether this is your second Kiersten Modglin novel or your 30th, I hope it was everything you wished for and nothing like you expected.

ABOUT THE AUTHOR

KIERSTEN MODGLIN is an Amazon Top 10 bestselling author of psychological thrillers and a member of International Thriller Writers, Novelists, Inc., and the Alliance of Independent Authors. Kiersten is a KDP Select All-Star and a recipient of *ThrillerFix*'s Best Psychological Thriller Award and *Suspense Magazine*'s Best Book of 2021 Award. She grew up in rural western Kentucky and later relocated to Nashville, Tennessee, where she now lives with her husband, daughter, and their two Boston terriers: Cedric and Georgie. Kiersten's work is currently being translated into multiple languages and readers across the world refer to her as 'The Queen of Twists.' A Netflix addict, Shonda Rhimes superfan, psychology fanatic, and *indoor* enthusiast, Kiersten enjoys rainy days spent with her nose in a book.

Sign up for Kiersten's newsletter here:
http://eepurl.com/b3cNFP
Sign up for text alerts from Kiersten here:
www.kierstenmodglinauthor.com/textalerts.html

www.kierstenmodglinauthor.com
www.facebook.com/kierstenmodglinauthor
www.facebook.com/groups/kmodsquad
www.twitter.com/kmodglinauthor
www.instagram.com/kierstenmodglinauthor
www.tiktok.com/@kierstenmodglinauthor
www.goodreads.com/kierstenmodglinauthor
www.bookbub.com/authors/kiersten-modglin
www.amazon.com/author/kierstenmodglin

ALSO BY KIERSTEN MODGLIN

STANDALONE NOVELS

Becoming Mrs. Abbott

The List

The Missing Piece

Playing Jenna

The Beginning After

The Better Choice

The Good Neighbors

The Lucky Ones

I Said Yes

The Mother-in-Law

The Dream Job

The Liar's Wife

My Husband's Secret

The Perfect Getaway

The Arrangement

The Roommate

The Missing

Just Married

Our Little Secret

Widow Falls

Missing Daughter

The Reunion

Tell Me the Truth

The Dinner Guests

ARRANGEMENT NOVELS

The Arrangement (Arrangement Novels, #1)

The Amendment (Arrangement Novels, #2)

The Atonement (Arrangement Novels, #3)

THE MESSES SERIES

The Cleaner (The Messes, #1)

The Healer (The Messes, #2)

The Liar (The Messes, #3)

The Prisoner (The Messes, #4)

NOVELLAS

The Long Route: A Lover's Landing Novella

The Stranger in the Woods: A Crimson Falls Novella

THE LOCKE INDUSTRIES SERIES

The Nanny's Secret

CPSIA information can be obtained
at www.ICGtesting.com
Printed in the USA
LVHW041640260623
750807LV00003B/597

9 781956 538211